FAKE FIANCE

A BILLIONAIRE SECOND CHANCE ROMANCE

TARA CRESCENT

Text copyright © 2017 Tara Crescent
All Rights Reserved

No part of this book may be reproduced in any form or by any electronic or mechanical means including information storage and retrieval systems, without permission in writing from the author. The only exception is by a reviewer, who may quote short excerpts in a review.

This book is a work of fiction. Names, characters, places, and incidents either are products of the author's imagination or are used fictitiously. Any resemblance to actual persons, living or dead, events, or locales is entirely coincidental.

My editor Jim takes the comma-filled words that emerge from my keyboard and shapes it into a story worth reading. As always, my undying gratitude.

Additional thanks for Miranda's laser-sharp eyes.

FREE STORY OFFER

Get a free story when you subscribe to <u>my mailing list!</u>

Boyfriend by the Hour
This steamy, romantic story contains a dominant hero who's pretending to be an escort, and a sassy heroine who's given up on real relationships.

Sadie:

I can't believe I have the hots for an escort.

Cole Mitchell is ripped, bearded, sexy and dominant. When he moves next door to me, I find it impossible to resist sampling the wares.

But Cole's not a one-woman kind of guy, and I won't share.

Cole:

She thinks I'm an escort. I'm not.

I thought I'd do anything to sleep with Sadie. Then I realized I want more. I want Sadie. Forever.

I'm not the escort she thinks I am.

Now, I just have to make sure she never finds out.

FAKE FIANCE

One week with the man I never got over. One week where I pose as his fiancée. One week where I act like I'm madly in love with him. *I can survive that.*

Maddie Morland. *My shining star.*

She's the only woman I've ever loved.
The only woman I can't get out of my mind.

Now, nine years later, she's back.
She needs money. I need a fiancée.

I tell myself that all I want is closure.
But things have never been that simple where Maddie's concerned…

Cameron Drake.

He was always too good for me.
My mother was a drunk. My father was in jail.

Cameron was my refuge. My escape. *Until his father drove me away.*

But now?
Cameron's a billionaire. Sexier than ever.
He wants to pretend we're engaged. *Wants me to pretend I'm still in love with him.*
Except I won't be pretending…

1

CAMERON

"You're a stubborn son of a bitch, you know that, Cameron?"

Brent Roberts, the man who's spoken those words, is something of a sore loser. He inherited his media company from his father, and in the five years he's been the CEO, he's done his level best to run it into the ground. He's lucky I'm interested in buying it, and despite what he thinks, I've offered to pay a fair price.

I shrug. "If you think you can do better elsewhere, you're free to walk away."

He glares at me and I stare back. Truth is, I have no use for men like Roberts. He's lazy and unfocused; he's never done an honest day's work in his life.

Roberts caves, as I expect him to. "Fine," he mutters sullenly. "Let's get this deal done."

Debra Marks, my second in command, conceals her triumphant grin as Roberts signs on the dotted line. When the team of lawyers clear out of my office, she thrusts her fist in the air in a victorious gesture. "What a fool," she smirks.

"He has the best team in the country, and he doesn't know it. We'll make much better use of Pulse Media."

"Indeed." I walk over to the bar in the corner of my office and pour her a drink. "You did good on this deal, Deb."

She accepts it with a smile of thanks. "You flatter me, boss. It wasn't my negotiating skills that sealed the deal."

I slosh some top-shelf whiskey into a glass, and raise it in Deb's direction. The Pulse Media deal has taken months of hard work and preparation. I've earned this celebration.

"Any summer vacation plans?" Deb asks as we sip our drinks. "You typically head to Muskoka this time of the year, don't you?"

It's practically a Canadian rite of passage to go away to the family cottage during summer. Deb has no idea that her innocent question sends a sharp stab of pain through my heart. Even now. *Even after all these years.*

I haven't seen or heard from Maddie in almost a decade. She was offered a choice between money and love, and she chose the cash and broke my heart.

I wonder where she is now.

"If I can get away," I hedge. "What about you, Deb? That husband of yours whisking you off somewhere good?"

"Nah," she replies. "I like Toronto in the summer. We'll go away when it gets colder. We're planning a trip to Greece in the fall."

There's a knock on the door, and my assistant Kelli sticks her head in. "You have a visitor, Mr. Drake," she stammers. "It's your grandfather. I know he doesn't have an appointment, but…"

Poor Kelli. She has no desire to get in the middle of a family feud, and I don't blame her. "That's okay, Kelli, I'll see him." I gulp down the rest of my drink as Deb gets up to leave. "Have a good weekend, Cam," she says. "See you Monday."

I HAVEN'T SEEN my grandfather in a few months. He's a difficult man to love, strict and unyielding. He enters my office now, giving the bottle of whiskey on the table a disapproving look. "Drinking on the job? Is this what passes as work nowadays?" he demands.

I refuse to be drawn into this discussion. "Hello to you too, grandfather. To what do I owe the pleasure of your company?"

He sits down opposite me, grunting as he folds himself into his seat. That noise, a small admittance of weakness, startles the crap out of me. Through my adolescence, my grandfather has been such a larger than life presence that I've failed to realize he's getting old. He's in his eighties now. He's not going to live very much longer.

I straighten the pieces of paper at my desk to avoid confronting that thought. The silence between us grows. He breaks it first. "I was in the neighborhood," he says, "and I thought I'd come and see if you were planning to come to the cottage this year. I left a message for you, but you haven't replied."

Every year, my family gets together for one week in the summer. Seven days of seething resentments, angst and dysfunction. My father will be there, ready to pitch some crackpot scheme to my grandfather. His sister, my aunt Emily, will be there, patient and smiling, trying to smooth over the various squabbles that tend to break out when we're around each other. My uncle Colt died when I was a teenager, but his four sons typically attend. Of course, we never talk about my estranged uncle Julian, and we do our level best to pretend that branch of the family doesn't exist.

The family drama isn't the only reason I don't want to go. Every time I go to the cottage, it reminds me of Maddie. Every time I sit on the dock, I can't help remembering the times I slathered sunscreen on her velvet skin. Every time I swim in the lake, memories of her laughter haunt me.

Even now. Even after all these years.

Summer after summer, I go back to the cottage, observing the Drake family traditions, though all I feel is pain. The wound is still there, and being at the cottage just lances it open.

This year, I'm going to stay away. I'm going to remain in the city where there are fast women and faster cars, and an infinite number of distractions, and I'm going to let Maddie go, once and for all. "I haven't made up my mind," I lie.

He frowns. "It's probably going to be the last summer you'll get to spend there," he says. "I'm selling the cottage."

At that, I sit up. The huge, rambling farmhouse has been in my grandfather's family for generations. More than that, it's my aunt Emily's home. Why he suddenly wants to get rid of it, I have no idea. It isn't for the money--he has plenty of it. "You're selling the place?" I ask carefully. "To whom?"

"Ryder's interested," he replies.

Shock courses through me. Ryder is Uncle Julian's son. I had no idea my grandfather was even in contact with him. "And you're entertaining his offer?" I ask carefully. "What about Emily? This is her home you're talking about."

I've only met Ryder once, at a party in Toronto a few months ago. He seemed like a good-enough guy, very much in love with his wife, Zoe.

If it weren't for Aunt Emily, I wouldn't care that Ryder wants to buy the cottage. But my aunt loves the cottage. It's her home, damn it. She spends all her time there, even in the cold winter months, lost in memories of happier days.

"I'll find Emily another place to live," my grandfather replies dismissively. "I want the cottage to go to a Drake, and Ryder's the only one in your generation who seems to be interested in children. His wife is pregnant." His knuckles grip the armrests of the chair he's sitting on. "I have six grandchildren. You. Ryder. Noah. Zachary. Declan. Liam. And Ryder's the only one who's settled down."

"Seven," I correct him. "You have seven grandchildren. You forgot Ryder's sister Gigi."

His lips curl with distaste. "I refuse to count Julian's illegitimate daughter."

"Of course. Because it's Gigi's fault that your son couldn't keep it in his pants."

He flinches. "I demand to be spoken to with respect," he says through clenched teeth.

I refrain from rolling my eyes. It's not like I'm learning anything new about my grandfather. Edward Drake only cares about the family name. Emily has no children, and even if she did, they wouldn't be Drakes. Because of that, she's getting tossed out of her home and Ryder, who is a near-stranger, will move in.

My aunt is the only member of my family that I love without reservation. She has a heart of gold. She'll never say anything about being forced to leave the cottage, but she'll be miserable. To keep her happy, I would do anything.

"You're selling to Ryder because his wife is pregnant?" I straighten another piece of paper on my desk, thinking quickly. There's no point offering to beat Ryder's price; my grandfather will only dig in his heels harder. And there's no point trying to appeal to his heart; Emily was eighteen when she sneaked out to go to a party with her boyfriend, and got into the accident that damaged her spine and left her in a wheelchair. My grandfather still hasn't forgiven her for breaking his rules and leaving home without permission.

I can't produce a pregnant wife, but I can do the next best thing. I can show up to Muskoka with a fiancée. I can be obviously, visibly in love. My grandfather barely knows Ryder; it'll be enough to change his mind about selling the family cottage to my estranged cousin. "In that case, I'll be there," I continue. "Also, I'm bringing someone."

"You are?" His eyes light up, and I wince inwardly. *Lying to an old man, Cameron? Even for you, that's low.* "You've never brought anyone to the cottage."

Except for Maddie. Of course, Maddie was from the wrong side of the tracks, and my grandfather and my father like to pretend she didn't exist. I'm not surprised Edward Drake doesn't mention her now.

I double-down on the lie. "Yes. I'm seeing someone and it's serious. You'll meet her next week."

"It's about time," he says, slowly rising to his feet. "You're thirty-one. When I was your age, I'd already been married for eleven years."

And he'd had four children, three sons and a daughter, and of the four of them, only two are alive. Things haven't been easy for Edward Drake.

I feel a surge of sympathy for the old man and another stab of guilt at the lie I'm telling him. Then I remember his casual dismissal of Aunt Emily, and my resolve hardens. I intend to buy the cottage and make sure my aunt lives in it for the rest of her life.

He moves toward the door, then turns back, a stiff smile on his face. "I'm delighted to hear that you've found someone, Cameron." He hesitates for an instant, then continues with a look of resolution on his face. "I'm looking forward to meeting your girlfriend. And if you're getting married and are interested in the property..."

His voice trails off, his meaning clear. If my grandfather is convinced I'm in a serious relationship, I have a shot at getting the cottage. If not, he'll sell it to Ryder.

The family vacation is next week.

I have seven days to find a woman that is crazy enough to pretend to be madly in love with me and smart enough to pull the wool over my family's eyes, and I don't know where to start looking.

2

MADDIE

"Maddie, your secret admirer is here." Jenna Andrews winks cheekily at me. "Someone has a crush on Maddie," she continues in a sing-song.

My cheeks heat. Jenna's voice has carried across the room, and the customer entering the coffee shop has clearly heard her.

Fan-*fucking*-tastic.

Jenna always does this. Every. Single. Week. My boss has visions of being a matchmaker. She's decided, along with my sister Misti, that I should end my dating drought and go out with the tall blond man.

"Will you shush?" I frown at Jenna, who grins back, unabashed, and moves aside to allow me to wait on the customer. My so-called secret admirer comes up to the counter. "Your friend's not subtle, is she?" he asks with a raised eyebrow.

I want to die. Or kill Jenna. Either one. "Ignore her," I mutter, unable to meet the guy's eyes. "What can I get you?"

"Tall coffee please," he says. "No milk, no sugar, though I wouldn't say no to a chocolate chip cookie."

"Coming right up."

I pour the coffee into a cup and put the cookie on a plate, my thoughts elsewhere. Jenna's been trying to get me to date for months, insisting that there's something wrong with my extreme disinterest in men.

She's probably right. Had she tried to set me up nine years ago, when I first moved to Calgary, I would have cooperated with her agenda.

Of course, nine years ago, my heart had been shredded to pieces by Cameron Drake, and I was desperate to heal it. I'm wiser now. I've tried dating. I even had a boyfriend once, though it didn't survive the two-month mark.

The heat, the fire, the passion I had with Cam... that's gone forever. And all of Jenna's subtle-as-a-hammer matchmaking can't change that.

"So," the man says. "*Would* you like to go out sometime?"

I can see Jenna out of the corner of my eye. She's doing a gleeful little hip wiggle, her signature celebration move. Oh dear. She's really not going to like my answer. "I'm sorry," I tell the guy regretfully. "I don't date."

"At all?" he asks, his eyebrows rising. "Or just me?"

"At all." I soften the sting of my rejection with a small smile. "Sorry."

He shrugs. "Nothing ventured, nothing gained." He opens his wallet to pay for his drink, and hands me a ten-dollar bill and a business card. "If you change your mind, you know how to reach me."

I watch him leave, but I'm not seeing him. I'm seeing a tall, broad-shouldered man, with dark hair and stubble grazing his cheek. Eyes that change from stormy gray to the clearest blue, depending on his mood. I'm seeing the only man I was ever in love with, the man I ran away from. Cameron Drake.

"Oh my god." At my side, Jenna examines the card I'm holding, her eyes wide. "That's Drew Knight."

"Who?"

"Drew Knight. Owns half the oil fields in Canada. Richest guy in Calgary. Do you not pay attention, Maddie?" Her voice rises in a shrill pitch of excitement. "Oh my god, Drew Knight asked you out, and you said no."

"I'm not interested," I reply, handing her the card. "You call him."

AT NINE AT NIGHT, the coffee shop is deserted. I'm preparing to close up when my phone rings. *Must be Misti*, I think, but the voice on the other end isn't my eighteen-year old sister.

"Madison Morland?" A woman asks tentatively. "My name is Irene Kirkland. I'm calling from St. Michael's Hospital. I'm so sorry to be the bearer of bad news, but your mother passed away a few hours ago from a heroin overdose."

The news *shouldn't* take me by surprise. Given my mother's long history of drug and alcohol abuse, I *should* have been prepared for this phone call.

I'm not. My throat closes and grief overtakes me. Angie Morland was a horrible mother, but she was the only mother I had.

"Madison?" she repeats. "Are you there?"

"Yeah." I find the words with difficulty. "Sorry." My mind races. I'll have to arrange a funeral and figure out how to pay for it. My mom had driven away most of her friends with her substance abuse problem, but people will still need to be notified.

I can't do all of that from Calgary. I'm going to have to go back to Ontario. The province I haven't set foot in for nine long years.

Ms. Kirkland kindly gives me the names of some inexpensive funeral homes, and I scribble them down on a roll of receipt tape, still in a daze. It'll take me two long days to drive back to Toronto. Misti might not want to go to the funeral, but I'll have to tell her. My dad might want to know, but even if I wanted to talk to him, I don't know how to reach him. The last I heard, he'd been arrested again.

I have to call Jenna. Ask for a week off. I chew on my knuckle absently as I contemplate if my bank balance will survive the strain. Misti's going to need money for textbooks in the fall, and I was counting on a good summer of tips to be able to pay for them.

My mother's dead.

The world seems to slow down. I blink my tears away. I can't cry, not now. There's too many things that need to be done before I go back home.

Home. Toronto.

I remember the day I'd left far too well. It was a beautiful sunny day, but I'd seen none of it. I'd just left Cameron, slipping away without saying goodbye. Knowing that there was nothing to be said. Nothing that needed to be said. I'd been in tears as I went back to my mother's apartment. She was passed out on the couch, an empty bottle of rye on the floor next to her. Sitting in a corner was Misti, struggling to ignore the desolation in front of her so she could finish her homework.

I'd known then that I had to take her away. It was too late for me; I was always going to be branded as the girl whose mother was a junkie and whose father was in jail. But Misti's life could be different. She could go to college, make something of herself.

I left my mother a note explaining what I was going to do, and we drove away. There were jobs in Calgary, so we headed west.

Two days later, my mother called me, angry and bitter, telling me she never wanted to see either of us again.

Now she's dead.

I should call Misti, but I need to build up my courage for that. With shaking hands, I dial Jenna. When she picks up, I quickly explain the situation. "Of course you can take time off," she says at once. "Maddie, I'm so sorry."

"I'm leaving you in the lurch." Jenna has saved money for years to be able to start her own business. I feel terrible about abandoning her.

"Of course not," she scoffs. "It's summer. Peter doesn't have any classes, so he's been begging me for more hours. We'll be fine, Maddie. Don't worry about us. Take all the time you need."

Jenna knows the circumstances of my departure from Toronto, my estrangement from my family. Her voice softens in sympathy. "How are you feeling?"

"I don't know." Words are difficult. "It hasn't sunk in yet."

"Is there anything I can do? Do you need money?"

That's Jenna for you. She'd give you the shirt off her back with a smile on her face. A lump rises in my throat. "I'll manage." I don't know how--funerals aren't cheap-- but I'll figure it out.

Once I hang up, I stare blankly at the counter. *I have to tell Misti.*

It's the last week of college. Misti's done with her finals.

She's probably partying with her friends right now. I should let her enjoy herself.

You can't put this moment off, Maddie.

I take a deep breath and call her. Her phone rings once, twice. On the third ring, she picks up. The loud music in the background tells me I was right; she's at a party. "Maddie," she yells, screaming to be heard over the noise. "I'm so sorry, I totally forgot to call you."

I should find a gentle way of breaking the news, but the words tumble out of my mouth before I can stop them. "Mom's dead."

"Oh." She pauses. "Did she overdose?"

I squeeze my eyes shut. "Yeah. She did, sweetie."

There's a false hardness in my baby sister's voice. "She had it coming," she says.

I know Misti. She's hurting, but she won't show it. She's tough. You had to be tough to survive growing up in our house. "I'm leaving tomorrow morning to drive to Toronto." I gulp. "I have to make the funeral arrangements."

"I'll come with you."

"You will?" I didn't expect this.

"Yeah," she replies. "It's a long drive. You shouldn't have to do it alone." She swallows. "I won't let you do it alone."

We're not talking about the drive anymore; we both know it. We're talking about saying goodbye to a woman who rarely loved us, who made us cry so much more than she made us smile.

My throat feels sore, scratchy. "Thanks, baby," I tell her softly. "I'll pick you up at seven, okay?"

On a normal day, Misti would have whined about our early start, but this isn't a normal day. "Okay, Maddie," she says. "See you then."

3

CAMERON

Six days later, I'm no closer to finding a woman to be my fake fiancée.

It's Thursday evening. The sun is low in the sky when I leave work. I make my way to my car, a cherry-red 1973 Porsche Carrera that I bought at auction last year for an absolutely obscene sum of money. *Worth every penny,* I think as I turn the key in the ignition and the motor revs to life with a muted roar. *I love this car.*

Traffic is lighter than usual, people leaving the city ahead of the long weekend, hoping to avoid the traffic on the 400. I drive home, my thoughts all over the place. I shouldn't have told my grandfather I was bringing someone to the cottage. The news has made its rounds in my family. My father left a message for me over the weekend, demanding to know who the woman is, which is a bit rich of him given that we barely tolerate each other.

A familiar tune fills the air. *Come As You Are*, the acoustic version. As Kurt Cobain sings the first note, I'm pulled into the past.

"I'm nervous about this week, Cam." Maddie turns to me, her hazel eyes filled with worry. *"What if everyone hates me?"*

Even when she's frowning, Maddie's gorgeous. "It is impossible to hate you, Madison Morland," I tell her, my hand closing around her fingers. "You have nothing to worry about."

She gnaws on her lower lip. "Your dad doesn't like me," she mutters.

"Fuck him. He's just being a snob."

"Damn it, Cam." She exhales in exasperation, pulling her hand away from mine. "Will you take me seriously?"

I look into her face and feel like a heel. Her eyes are swimming with tears. "Maddie," I say helplessly. My smart, sweet, kind girlfriend doesn't believe she belongs in my world, and I don't know how to tell her that she is my world. There's nothing in my life that matters to me as much as she does. The moment I laid eyes on her, laughing with her teammates at a swim meet, I knew we belonged together. "Listen to me. I love you. I promise I won't leave your side all week, okay?"

"Really?" Her tone is hopeful.

"Cross my heart and hope to die," I tell her solemnly. "Now, open the glove box. I got you a present."

Her smile lights up the car. "A present? You didn't have to."

"I wanted to." I watch as she unwraps the Nirvana Unplugged CD. It's her favorite band, but she doesn't own a single album of theirs.

"Oh Cam, it's perfect." She sounds so happy. "Can we play it now?"

I was crazy about her. I thought I was the luckiest guy in the world. I knew, deep in my heart, that she was the woman I was going to spend the rest of my life with.

I'd been wrong. Four days after that conversation, she'd

taken the fifty thousand dollars my dad gave her to leave me alone, and she'd left my life forever.

AFTER DINNER, I sit outside in my backyard, reading the local paper. There's a festival this weekend in my neighborhood, and I want to know what streets will be closed as a result. I'm flipping through the sheets, trying to find the information I want, when a photo catches my eye. It's Angie Morland, Maddie's mother.

The article is brief. Angela Morland was found in her apartment, passed out from a heroin overdose. She was given two doses of Narcan at the scene and rushed to St. Michael's, but didn't survive.

My hand reaches for my phone before my mind catches up. I dial Roman Barrett, the detective I use when I need information, fast. "I need the funeral details for an Angela Morland," I tell him when he answers. "She died at St. Michael's earlier this week."

"Give me fifteen minutes," he replies. I hear the sound of music and laughter in the background, signs that Barrett isn't in his Yorkville office. Still, the man is never without his laptop.

Ten minutes later, he calls me back with an answer. "There was a cremation this afternoon," he says, "and a memorial tonight." He gives me an address in the west end of the city. "It started twenty minutes ago. If you want to attend, you better drive quickly."

THERE ARE ONLY a handful of cars in the parking lot. I screech to a halt and rush in. The sign at the front informs me that the Angela Morland memorial is upstairs, in Room 2B.

My heart beats in my chest as I climb the stairs. I can't deny that I'm hoping to see Maddie.

It's been nine years, Cameron. She might be married. She might even have children.

I stop cold as that realization sweeps over me, then I force myself to continue to put one foot in front of another.

Room 2B is almost empty. Standing in the small hallway, I look inside. There's only three people there. Maddie, another woman who looks to be in her early twenties, wearing jeans and a black t-shirt, and a man with a frown on his face.

I barely notice the other people. I'm too busy drinking in the sight of Maddie. Then the conversation continues, and I stop to pay attention, because something is wrong.

"Ms. Morland," the man is saying to Maddie. "I know how difficult this is, and I apologize for the timing. Unfortunately, your credit card was declined."

I stand to one side and listen in, my brain struggling to process the scene. The funeral home is shabby. There are no tables of food and drink, just a small plate of cookies. Maddie's drawn the guy aside, away from the other woman, and is offering him another credit card, her face shrouded with anxiety.

She's in trouble.

"Cameron?" The woman wearing jeans speaks my name loudly, an expression of surprise on her face. "Is that you?"

"Misti." Maddie's baby sister. I can't believe I didn't recognize her. I walk into the room and the young woman envelops me in a hug. "You're all grown up now."

Maddie looks up sharply. When her eyes meet mine, she turns pale. "Cameron," she whispers.

"Hello Maddie." I'm proud of how even my voice is. "Long time no see."

SHE SWAYS on her feet and slumps into a chair. I lurch toward her in concern, instinctively, automatically, the nine years melting away in an instant, and then I realize what I'm doing and stop myself.

Her hair's different, longer. She used to wear it short-- *it's too hard to bundle up under a swim cap, Cam,* she would say with a laugh when I suggested she grow it. It tumbles in shiny waves over her shoulders. It suits her. She's even more beautiful now, if such a thing is possible. Her full lips shimmer with some kind of gloss that makes me want to press my mouth against her and taste... Her curves make me think of sin, even in this place of mourning.

The man edges away. Maddie watches him leave, then gives me an unreadable look. "What are you doing here?" she asks, direct as ever.

"I came to see an old friend. We were friends once, weren't we?"

"Were we?" Her voice is cool. "I don't remember it that way."

I'm taken aback by her hostility. I can't understand it. She left me. I'm the one who should be furious.

I'm about to open my mouth to say something cold and cutting before I pivot on my heels and walk away, out of her life, forever. Then I stop myself, because Maddie's shredding a napkin in her hands, bits of paper falling in tiny pieces on her lap.

A tell I remember from the past.

Maddie isn't as unaffected by our encounter as she appears to be. She's trying to push me away. *Why?*

Misti's watching the two of us with a fascinated expression on her face. "I should give you guys some space," she says awkwardly. "I'll be waiting in the car, Maddie."

"There's no need," Maddie replies, glaring at me. "Thanks Misti," I say at the same time. I win the battle of wills, because Misti backs away, practically running down the stairs to escape the tension between us.

"What did you do that for?" she asks me crossly, a familiar fire in her eyes. This is the Madison Morland I fell in love with. "We have nothing to talk about."

Why did you leave me, Maddie? I would have given you everything I owned; you only had to ask.

"What was that guy saying?" I demand. "Your credit card was declined?"

Maddie needs money. I need to convince my family I'm serious about a woman. My subconscious has been working on a solution to my problem and she's standing in front of me, with an icy look on her face and a shredded napkin mess at her feet.

"You're stooping to eavesdropping now, Cam? Our conversation is none of your business. I can handle myself."

I need to get Maddie on board with my idea. "Have a drink with me." She starts to protest, and I hold up my hand. "One drink, Maddie. For old times' sake."

She gives me a long look, then she nods. "We're staying in a motel on Lakeshore tonight," she says. "There's a bar next to it."

"Okay."

This is madness, my brain tells me. *She broke your heart once. Stay away from her.*

I don't listen to that voice of caution. Instead, I follow Maddie downstairs.

4

MADDIE

Cameron Drake is here.

There are so many things I want to scream at him. *Why didn't you call me that night? Why did you never try to find me? And most importantly, why, after all these years, are you here now?*

He looks grown-up. His dark hair is cut shorter now. He's traded the torn jeans and faded t-shirts for a suit. He looks like the successful billionaire he is.

His eyes haven't changed. They're as blue as the lake on a clear summer afternoon, and when they meet mine, the years between us fall away.

He broke my heart nine years ago; I can't let it happen again.

We walk downstairs without a word. I feel his gaze burning a hole in my back. The silence lengthens and I have to break it. "The hotel is on Lakeshore," I say, babbling with nerves. "I'll drive there. You can follow me, okay?"

"Sure thing, Maddie."

I pass the funeral home office. Phil Earlscourt, the guy in charge, was upstairs earlier saying something about my credit card being declined. I'd handed him a different card, but I don't know what's going on. There should have been enough room on my credit for the cremation. It should have gone through. First thing tomorrow morning, I have to sort that out.

God, I'm tired. The thirty-six hour drive from Calgary, seeing my mother's wasted body--I'm completely drained. I'm not ready to deal with Cameron. My defenses are down.

Things used to be so good between us.

There's a bright red Porsche in the parking lot. Even in the dusk, I can see the gleam of the paint on the classic car. "Yours, I assume? I'm surprised you left it unattended in this neighborhood."

"I was preoccupied with other things," he replies blandly. He walks me to my car and opens the driver's side door for me, his eyes resting on the empty coffee cups in the back seat. "Long drive?"

"I live in Calgary now," I reply shortly, answering the unasked question.

"You drove from Calgary?" he demands. "In this piece of shit? When did you get in?"

"Earlier this afternoon," I say through my teeth, bristling at his cutting dismissal of my car. "What's with the questions, Cam?"

"You must be exhausted." His gaze is sharp. "You shouldn't be driving."

"It doesn't matter," I snap. *Who died and made him my keeper?*

"Yes, it does," he says grimly. "I'm not letting you get behind the wheel."

Warmth that he cares about me wars with my ire about being told what to do. Misti watches from the passenger seat, avidly curious. I groan inwardly. The last thing I want is an audience, even if it's just my sister. "Fine," I sigh. "Let's do it your way."

Cam's on his phone. "Drake here," he says. "I need a car and a spare driver." He rattles off the address and hangs up. "I'd drive the two of you myself, but the car's a two-seater."

"Of course," I say snidely. "Gorgeous and impractical. Just like its owner."

His lips curl into a slow grin. "You think I'm gorgeous, Maddie?" His voice lowers an octave. "I'm flattered, babe."

That voice. Sexy as sin, tempting me, teasing me. It shouldn't affect me, not after all these years, but it does. It's not fair that my blood hums with need and longing for what used to be, and he's standing in front of me, calm and collected.

While we wait for the car service to show up, Cam and Misti make small talk. It doesn't take long before a black Bentley pulls into the parking lot. Two men jump out and greet Cameron deferentially. "Sorry about the delay, Mr. Drake," one of them apologizes. "Traffic was murder."

"No worries, Paul," Cameron says easily. "Can one of you drive this car home," he gestures to my clunker, which looks even shabbier than usual next to the beautiful Porsche and the swanky Bentley, "and the other take Ms. Morland and her sister to their hotel? I'll follow you."

I SINK into the sumptuous leather of the backseat. Misti slides in next to me. Once we're off, she turns to me with a serious look on her face. "Are you okay, Maddie?" she asks me softly. "Seeing Cameron again has got to be a shock."

The driver has closed the partition between the front and the back so we can have some privacy. "I'll live," I reply shortly. I don't want to talk about my former boyfriend. The memories are too painful.

"I never asked you why you guys broke up. You were so crazy about him. Did he cheat on you?"

"What?" I give Misti a shocked look. "Why would you think that?"

"You ended things so abruptly. I couldn't think of any other reason you'd do that."

I close my eyes. Nine years ago, I'd been intensely aware about the gulf between Cameron Drake's world and mine. His family was among Canada's wealthiest; my mother was a junkie and my father was about to be released from prison. It felt like a chasm that couldn't be crossed.

It's easier to let Misti believe that Cameron cheated than to explain the truth. Easier than telling her while it had been too late for me, I'd taken her away from our chaotic lives in Toronto so that she could have a fresh start, away from our parents.

Except I can't do it.

"He didn't cheat." In the year we'd been together, I never doubted that he loved me, not even for an instant. *Until I left and he never called.* "He wouldn't cheat. That's not who Cameron is."

She doesn't press me about why we broke up. Perhaps she hears the quiver in my voice. She leans back in her seat, and stares into the distance. "I need to tell you something," she whispers. "All the way here, I've been waiting for the right moment..." She swallows. "I lost my swimming scholarship."

"What?"

Her face is etched with misery. "I'm so sorry, Maddie. I know how much you wanted me to go to college. But the truth is, I'm not that good a swimmer, not like you. I'm struggling to qualify at meets. The coach told me last week that they're not going to be renewing my stipend." There's a tremble in her voice. "I'm sorry I've disappointed you."

"Oh sweetie." I fold her into a hug. "You've never disappointed me in your life. Don't worry about the scholarship. We'll figure out how to pay for tuition. Everything's going to be okay."

My words are reassuring, but my heart is filled with despair. I'm barely surviving as it is. I have no idea where I'm going to find the extra thousands of dollars I need to pay for Misti's university education.

THE CAR PULLS into the motel parking lot we're staying at. I survey the low-slung building with doubt. It looked good enough on the Internet, but now that we're here, I'm having second thoughts. There's a half-dozen young men hanging out in the immediate vicinity, smoking weed, and their gazes rest a little too long on Misti's long legs as she heads to the office to get our room key.

Cameron's Porsche roars to a stop next to me. He unfolds himself from his car and gives the place a once-over. "You're not staying here," he says flatly.

"Give it a rest, Cam," I tell him wearily. The bed probably has bedbugs, and I don't care. I just want to fall into oblivion and be done with this day. "Not all of us are billionaires, okay? This is what I can afford."

He runs his hand through his hair. "Maddie, this place isn't safe. I'll never forgive myself if something were to happen to you here. Stay at my place tonight. Please?"

It's the *please* that undoes me. Cameron doesn't usually ask. He demands.

"Okay." I give in for the second time. "Thank you."

An hour later, Misti and I have been shown to two luxurious bedrooms in Cameron's Forest Hill mansion, I've taken a hot shower and washed the road grime off my body, and I feel much more human. Pulling on a pair of shorts and a t-shirt, I leave my room and go in search of our host.

He's in the kitchen, opening a bottle of wine. "It's a lovely night," he says, his eyes lingering over my legs. "Let's drink this in the garden?"

I shrug. "You've been bossing me around all night," I mutter sarcastically. "Why stop now?"

He tips his head to one side and surveys me. "If my memory serves me correctly, you enjoyed being bossed around," he says silkily. "Have your tastes in bed changed in the last nine years?"

I inhale sharply. He *would* go there. "My tastes in bed are none of your business." I keep my tone even with difficulty. I thought I was over the hurt and the anger, but seeing Cameron has brought it all back. He was so upset that I left his family cottage early that he threw away our relationship. Nine years later, I'm still haunted by the way we ended.

He grabs two wine glasses from a cabinet and the bottle of Cabernet Sauvignon, and I follow him outside through the large glass patio doors that separate his kitchen from his backyard. A massive pool takes up half the space. Cameron still swims, obviously. "Your house suits you," I tell him, looking back at the sleek, modern wood and glass structure.

"I'm not sure if I'm getting complimented or insulted." He fills a glass and hands it to me, and I sink into a comfortable wicker chair. "I'm sorry about your mother. Did you see her often?"

"I haven't seen her in nine years."

He gives me a sharp look. "Why not?"

"I called her a terrible role-model and took Misti away to Calgary. She didn't like facing the truth."

He's surveying me in a way that's making me nervous. "Nine years ago? When did you move to Calgary?"

Less than twenty-hours after your father told me I was a liability and if I cared for you at all, I should get out of your life.

I don't answer his question. "Why are we here, Cam?" I ask abruptly. "Why did you want to have a drink? Nine years ago, you made your choice and I made mine. There's no point rehashing the past."

"I have a proposition for you."

Wariness prickles through me. "What kind of proposition?"

He contemplates his glass. "You remember my aunt Emily?"

I nod. She'd been the only member of Cameron's family who'd been kind to me. Everyone else had made me feel like an outsider, but Emily had been warm, engaging me in conversation about swimming and track, asking me what kind of books I liked to read and sharing her favorites with me. "Yes."

"Aunt Emily loves our family cottage, but my grandfather has decided to sell it to a cousin." He sounds annoyed. "My grandfather has a soft spot for family, and Ryder's wife is pregnant."

"That sucks." I'm not sure what he wants me to do about the situation.

"I could convince my grandfather to sell the place to me," he says. "If my grandfather thinks I'm in a serious relationship, he'll change his mind about letting Ryder buy the cottage."

A shiver of unease passes through me. I don't like where

this is going. "You can't mean..." My voice trails off. This is insane.

"I want you to pretend to be my fiancée for a month." He takes a sip of his wine, calm despite upending my world. "I'll pay you, of course. Does five hundred thousand seem reasonable?"

My head snaps up in shock. "Are you crazy?" *Five hundred thousand dollars.* My thoughts race. I won't have to worry about Misti's college education. I could buy a more reliable car. Pay for my mother's funeral without splitting the balance between five credit cards.

"I'm never crazy." He leans forward, his blue eyes meeting mine. "One month, Maddie. What about it?"

I look at him helplessly, desperate for an alternative to Cameron's proposal. One month with Cameron, pretending to be madly in love with him. I can't do it. This man crushed my heart nine years ago, and the scars still haven't faded.

"Say yes, Maddie." His voice lowers, deepens.

Think about Misti. You promised yourself that you'd give her a good life. She can't drop out of college.

"Yes." The words come out in a whisper.

"Good." His voice is brisk, efficient. "We leave for the cottage on Saturday morning. We'll go shopping tomorrow to get you what you need."

The cottage. The universe has a sick sense of humor. Of course we'll be going back to the place where things ended between Cameron and I.

I screw my eyes shut. *You're a survivor,* I tell myself, willing myself to believe it. *You'll be fine.*

5

CAMERON

This is not a second chance. This isn't an opportunity to go back and change the past.

Yet my heart hammers in my chest, and when I reach into my pocket for the ring, my hand trembles. "You'll need this." I reach for her finger.

She flinches when she sees what I'm holding. "You had a ring ready? Was I a foregone conclusion?" She's trying to be pert, but I can hear the unsteadiness in her voice.

"I've never taken you for granted, Mads."

I bought it nine years ago. I was passing an antique store and I'd seen the beautiful sapphire and diamond ring in the window and a voice had whispered in my ear, *Maddie would love this ring.*

This isn't the way I'd pictured giving it to her.

She gazes down at it for a long time, not saying a word. Finally, she looks up. "How've you been, Cameron?"

Ah, we're going to engage in small talk. I lean back. "Good. What about you, Maddie?"

She lifts her shoulder in a wry shrug. "I can't complain."

I fill her glass. "Is there someone you need to call in Calgary to explain that you won't be back for a month?"

Her lips curl up in a small smile. "Are you asking me if I'm dating someone?" She shakes her head. "I wouldn't have accepted your offer if I was in a relationship. What about you? No one in Toronto?"

The overwhelming relief I feel when I hear Maddie isn't dating anyone annoys me. This ruse is temporary. It's a ploy to get my grandfather to sell the cottage to me. *It isn't real.*

I rise to my feet abruptly. Sitting in the backyard under the moonlight, with only the quiet of the night to keep us company, my head is filled with memories of the past. Under the twinkling lights in my garden, her lips are soft and her cheeks are flushed. I want to pull her close to me, tear her clothes off her body and lose myself in her sweetness. I want to hear her soft gasps of pleasure; see the way she bites her lower lip as I surge into her. I want to kiss every inch of her body, make her writhe under me.

That's in the past. "I'm going to bed. See you in the morning."

MISTI WOLF-WHISTLES when she comes down for breakfast. "Nice bod, Cameron," she says, checking out my abs with a cheeky leer. "Is that for my sister's benefit?"

I grin back at her. Leaving Toronto has been good for Misti. I remember her as a too-thin kid with a constantly strained expression on her face. Now, she's a laughing young woman, comfortable in her own skin. "Help yourself to some coffee," I tell her. "Breakfast will be ready in ten minutes. You eat bacon, right?"

"I never met a pig I didn't love," she replies wryly.

"Are we still talking about bacon?"

She shrugs. There's something tense in her expression, something that suggests I shouldn't push. I change the subject. "I didn't get a chance yesterday to ask you how you've been."

"Really good." She opens a cabinet and finds a mug, and fills it to the brim with coffee. "Except for my mother dying, of course."

"Of course." I watch her curiously. "You don't seem upset."

She pushes her hair out of her eyes, and draws up a chair at the kitchen island. "My mother was a horrible person," she says matter-of-factly. "When she wasn't high on drugs, she was cruel, mean-spirited, and abusive. Maddie and I learned to fend for ourselves at a young age. I'm not going to pretend to be sad."

I hone in on the one word that causes my insides to sink. "Abusive?"

"Maddie never told you?" She looks up, surprised. "No, I guess she wouldn't have. You were her escape, you know."

It kills me that Maddie kept the worst of her home life hidden. We were a team, damn it. I would have done anything to keep her safe and happy.

Maddie enters the kitchen and gives her sister an astonished look. "Will wonders never cease," she marvels with a grin. "Misti's awake before me." She looks over in my direction, then averts her gaze. "Good morning," she says cautiously. "I didn't know you cooked."

"Just breakfast," I reply, fixing her a cup of coffee and handing it to her. "My housekeeper handles the bulk of the cooking."

"Of course." Her voice is neutral. She sits down next to her sister and clears her throat. "Misti, there's been a change in plans. I'm going to stick around in Toronto for a few weeks. I called Jenna last night and told her."

"Really?" Misti looks at Maddie, then at me, then at Maddie again. A smile breaks out on her face. "That's awesome, Mads. You work too hard. You deserve some time off."

Maddie looks tense. If I know her right, she's worrying about logistics. I step into the conversation before Maddie changes her mind about our deal. "Do you need to head back to Calgary in a hurry, Misti, or can you stick around with us?"

She shakes her head. "I can't stay, unfortunately. I have classes this summer, and a job that starts on Monday." She looks at Maddie questioningly. "I'll drive your car back Maddie, if that's okay with you?"

"That's a ridiculous idea," I reply instantly, even before Maddie has a chance to respond. "You can't drive across the country by yourself. I'll get you a plane ticket."

Maddie gives me a look of mingled gratitude and irritation. "I'll pay you back," she murmurs stiffly.

I roll my eyes. I don't want to spend all month squabbling with Maddie. "Can we fight after breakfast? I do better on a full stomach."

She chuckles reluctantly, then her gaze slowly travels down my naked chest, slowly, deliberately, and when her eyes stop at my groin, she exhales.

The blood rushes from my head. My cock turns to rock faster than I can blink.

I want to bend Maddie over the island and fuck her, deep and slow, until she's sobbing out my name, until her pussy's clenching around my dick, until she's delirious with pleasure.

Her kid sister is in the room, Cam.

"Bacon and eggs?" I ask them, thinking the most unsexy thoughts I can, of spreadsheets and merger proposals, until my erection subsides and I can join them at the island.

TWO HOURS LATER, we drop Misti off at the airport with a first class ticket to Calgary. Maddie hugs her sister goodbye and gets back into my Land Rover. "Thank you," she says, her voice soft. "That was very kind of you. Misti's super excited. She's never flown first-class before."

"She's a good kid." I put the car in drive. "You're not wearing your ring today."

"It's in my pocket." She fishes it out, wriggling in her seat as she does, and my cock stirs again. *Settle down,* I tell myself. If I'm going to get hard every time Maddie moves in the next month, I'm going to need a trip to the ER. "I didn't want Misti to know about our arrangement."

"Too complicated to explain?"

"Something like that," she replies, not meeting my eyes. "What's the plan for today? Do you have to work?"

"Unfortunately, yes." I need to stay away from Maddie as much as I can if I'm going to survive. "You're going to need clothes for the cottage. I've arranged for a car to take you shopping."

"Your family still dresses up for dinner?"

I give her a sidelong look, surprised. "You remember?"

"Every minute of that trip is seared into my brain," she replies flatly. "Apart from your grandfather and Emily, who else is going to be there?"

She'd been uncomfortable at the idea of meeting my family. She hadn't wanted to go, but I'd begged, pleaded and insisted, and she'd given in to make me happy. It had been a colossal mistake. Four days later, I was left to gaze on the wreckage of the most significant relationship of my life.

"My father," I reply. "Whichever trophy girlfriend he's currently seeing. Some friends of my grandfather. My cousin Noah."

"Trophy girlfriend?" Her eyebrow rises. "Are you really in a position to throw stones at your dad?"

My hands tighten on the steering wheel. "You're so ready to think the worst of me, aren't you, Maddie? I'm open and honest with the women I date. I don't lie to them, and I don't string them along. They don't show up at the houses of my friends and family in tears, wondering what they did wrong."

Her mouth twists. "I'm sorry," she says quietly. "I'm having a hard time letting go of the past."

I stare at the snarl of traffic in front of me. Judging by Misti's words this morning, Maddie did what she had to do to survive. I don't even blame her for taking my father's money--what else could she have done? Moving costs money, and Maddie never had any.

Yes, I wish things had been different, I wish that she'd asked me for help, trusted me instead of running away from me. But the past is the past, and revisiting it constantly isn't going to achieve anything. The next week is going to be difficult enough without us sniping at each other. Maddie's discomfort at meeting my family is obvious; her hands are twisted in her lap, crumpling and straightening the hem of her t-shirt. She's going to have to face my father, who paid her to leave me. And worst of all, the two of us are going to have to pretend to be in love with each other.

"Me too," I confess. "Shall we call a truce?"

She bites her lower lip again, and gives me a small nod.

"Do you still swim?" she asks, changing the topic. "Your pool is amazing."

More small talk. "I work out in a gym in winter, but there's nothing like an outdoor pool in summer. What about you?"

"My friend Jenna has a pool in her apartment building," she replies. "I try to swim there twice a week. Misti's really good, too. She had a scholarship to the University of Calgary."

I hear the pride in her voice, and underneath it, a certain wistfulness that she tries her best to hide. Maddie had planned to get a job after high school; university was not an option for someone who needed to support her family.

Again, my throat tightens at what could have been. Had she stayed, she would have wanted for nothing. I would have given her the sun and the moon and the stars, had she only asked.

Except she was too proud to ask for help. I was a blind fool for not seeing that then.

Nine years ago, when Maddie confessed she felt out of place in my world, I'd laughed away her concerns and told her I was crazy about her.

Nine years ago, I thought being in love was enough. But I was wrong and I lost her.

It's too late to change the past, but this time around, I can at least make sure she feels comfortable at the cottage. "Would you like me to come shopping with you?"

"Would you?" Her look of gratitude stops me cold. "I'm afraid I'll buy the wrong things."

There's a lump in my throat. I could have made things easier for her, and I didn't. I feel like slime. "Of course, Maddie," I tell her, keeping my tone light. "I'm especially going to enjoy helping you pick a swimsuit or two."

She laughs and punches my arm. "Some things haven't changed," she jokes.

"Hey, fair's fair. You eye-fucked me pretty thoroughly this morning. It seems only appropriate that I get to return the favor."

Her cheeks pinken. I wait for her to deny that she was checking me out, but she doesn't. Her gaze falls to her lap. "I'm still attracted to you," she whispers. "I was always attracted to you. When I saw you for the first time at the swim meet--for a minute--I couldn't breathe, you were that gorgeous. Then you came over and talked to me." A small smile plays about her lips as she remembers our first meeting. "I was tongue-tied and awkward, and my friends teased me about it. I wasn't interested in guys at school. Everything was about swimming. Until you came along."

She gives me a steady look. "You were my first, Cameron. There's a part of me that's always going to want you, okay? But I can't give in to that. You broke my heart once; I won't let you do it again. I'll pretend to be your fiancée. I'll pretend to be in love with you. But behind closed doors, all of that ends."

Every word she says is wise and probably right, but I'm not listening, because my attention is focused on one phrase. *I broke her heart?* I don't understand. She left me.

6

MADDIE

The rest of Friday is surprisingly fun. Both Cameron and I are determined not to talk about the past; that path will only lead to bitterness. We stick to the present, talking about music and books. Cameron bitches about the hole-filled plot of a thriller he's just finished; I wax eloquent about the sci-fi series I'm reading. He teases me about becoming a fan of the Calgary Flames, which I deny hotly. As futile as it might be, I'll remain a Leafs fan for life.

He's helpful with shopping. His driver takes us to a trendy Yorkville boutique that I'd never have the nerve to walk in on my own. There, Cameron turns me over to a saleswoman. "Jasmine will take care of you," he assures me, giving the grey-haired woman a smile that sets her swooning. "Jaz, my fiancée and I are heading to Port Carling for a week. She needs casual clothes, and a few dressier things to wear in the evening. And a swimsuit, of course."

His hand is wrapped around me in a proprietary gesture. *It's just for the sales lady,* I tell myself, trying not to melt with pleasure at his touch on my hip.

The sales woman's eyes widen when Cameron refers to me as his fiancée, and her eyes dart immediately to my left hand. "Of course, Mr. Drake," she says deferentially, giving me a curious look. Then she bustles into action. In less than an hour, she picks out shorts, t-shirts, cotton shirts, and some pretty dresses for the evening. When she catches a glance at my plain underwear, she clucks her tongue and adds a handful of lacy bras and panties. "Men are visual creatures," she chides. She convinces me to buy two swimsuits, a deep purple one-piece with flattering ruching at the sides, and a hot pink bikini.

I go along with all of it, pretending this is happening to someone else. My head spins with confusion.

I don't know what to make of Cameron.

This morning, when he poured my coffee, he remembered the way I take it. Nine years ago, the first time we'd gone out for breakfast together after making love all night, I'd ordered bacon and eggs and Cameron had teased me about my voracious appetite. This morning, he'd made the same meal. *Coincidence?* I don't know.

On the way back from the airport, he seemed surprised when I told him he'd broken my heart. I don't understand why he's confused. His father had confronted me and made me feel like I was using Cameron for his money. Unable to take it, I'd left Cameron a note explaining that I couldn't stay the entire week, and I'd fled back to Toronto.

And Cameron had chosen to let me go. He never contacted me. Naive me--I thought the worst that could happen was that we'd fight about my decision to leave. It had taken me days to realize he wasn't going to reach out to me.

"Nice swimsuit." Cameron's eyes darken with heat as I model the pink suit for him. I grin and twirl around, acutely aware that the saleswoman is watching us avidly. "We'll take it, Jaz." He hands her his credit card without taking his eyes off me.

She takes it and moves to the front register. "I should pay," I protest, though my attempt is pretty half-hearted. I caught a glimpse of a price tag on one of the sundresses, and nearly fainted. Six hundred and eighty-five dollars for a cotton dress.

"I thought we were deferring this fight," Cam replies, his gaze hungry. "Remember? Only on a full stomach?"

"Then take me to lunch. I'm starving."

"Me too," he murmurs. "Though it's not food that's going to satisfy my appetite."

"Cam..." *Don't do this. I can't resist you. I've never been able to resist you.* "We can't do this."

I'm almost at the point of tears. Something in my tone must alert him, because he nods. "You're right," he agrees easily. "Sorry, Maddie. I blame the swimsuit." He grins. "Go get changed, and I'll take you to this great Italian place I know, okay?"

After a very late lunch, Cameron locks himself in his office to work for a couple of hours. "I have to," he explains with an apologetic shrug. "Either I suck it up now, or I'll field calls and emails from my team all week."

"I have a book to read," I tell him. "I can entertain myself. And once I digest this meal, I'm going to give in to temptation and swim in your pool. If that's okay?"

"My house is yours, Maddie," he tells me, an odd look on his face.

If I didn't know better, I'd say he looks almost wistful.

ONCE CAMERON RETREATS into his upstairs office, I try

reading for a while, but I'm unable to focus. Instead, I get up and walk around, taking in Cam's house.

Last night, when I told him his place suited him, I was remarking on the overall feel of the place, clean and bright and modern. Now, I take in the details. Large canvases of modern art hang on the white walls, adding color and personality. The couches, covered in dark brown leather, look weathered. A red and orange throw is neatly folded and draped across the back of the sectional.

I used to tease him that it was easy for him to be tidy--he had a bunch of maids picking up after him. But that was just me busting his chops. Cameron was always neat.

This is insane, I tell myself. I need to stop being nostalgic about the past. Misti needs money for college, and that's the only reason I'm here.

WE DRIVE to the cottage the next morning. As I make my way to Cameron's Porsche, dressed in a flower-printed shirt and linen shorts that Jasmine picked for me yesterday, I'm almost sick with nerves. Cameron's family cottage in Muskoka was the setting of the most painful day of my life. If there was any way to avoid going...

"They don't bite, you know." Cam's voice is gentle.

"I like your aunt." *Your father is a poisonous viper and your grandfather is a snooty jerk.*

"And the rest of them are pretty awful. That's okay, you can say it. I have no illusions about my family." There's an underlying grimness in his voice. "Tell you what, I'll give you something to take your mind off the week."

"If you whip your dick out..." I tease him, "I'm going to take a very dim view of it." Okay, that's a total lie. I'd love to see him naked.

He laughs out loud. "God, I've missed you, Madison Morland. No one else says the things you do." He gives me a fond look. "I was going to ask you if you wanted to drive."

"This car? The Porsche? You're going to let me drive it?" My voice comes out in an astonished squeak.

In response, he holds his keys up to me. "Have at it, baby."

I gleefully snatch them away from him. "I'm not going to wait for you to change your mind." I get into the low-slung car, and pat the gearstick. "I'm going to take excellent care of you, baby," I croon to the car. "You're in good hands with me."

Cameron laughs again as he gets in. "I forgot that you talked to your car," he says. "I'm going to sound like a bit of a pussy, but please be careful."

I slant him an amused look as the engine roars to life. "How expensive was this Porsche, Cam?" I tease him. "Couple hundred grand? Don't worry. I'll be gentle."

He snorts. "Think a million," he retorts, then he winces. "Sorry. I just realized how that sounded. You must hate me."

"For being rich?" I give him a surprised look. "Why would I hate you for that?"

He goes quiet. "You're right," he says, after a long pause. "Money never did seem to matter to you, one way or the other, until the cottage."

I frown at him. *What does he mean, until the cottage?* I'm about to ask, then I decide not to. It's a lovely summer day. The sun shines in the sky, and there's not a cloud in sight. I don't want to ruin it. Until we arrive at the cottage, I intend to enjoy myself.

Cameron leans forward to fiddle with the radio, and I smack his hand away. "You know the rules," I tell him. "The driver gets to pick the station."

He smiles at me. "The Edge is featuring Nirvana all morning," he says. "What do you think, Maddie? For old times' sake?"

He remembers the songs I used to listen to. Be still, my heart. I ease the car into first and back out of Cameron's driveway. Kurt Cobain's voice fills the air, and I have to force myself not to be drawn into the past. It's unproductive, and besides, I'm driving a very expensive car. I need to pay attention to the road.

NINETY MINUTES LATER, we approach Barrie, at the turn off for Route 11. "Is that burger place still in Orillia?" I ask Cameron. "The one with the crazy lines?"

"It's more crowded than ever," he confirms. "Get off the highway and we'll stop there for lunch."

Some of my best dreams are about the burgers and fries I had on the way to Cameron's cottage. "You don't mind?"

His hand covers mine. "Of course not, Maddie. I want you to be happy."

"Well," I quip, doing my level best to ignore the spark that's coursing through my body at his touch, "I do love that burger."

As Cameron predicts, there's a long line outside the hamburger joint. "You need the bathroom, right?" he says indulgently. "Go ahead. I'll order for you. Burger with Swiss cheese and sautéed mushrooms, half onion-rings, half fries on the side, and a Coke. Right?"

I give him an exasperated look. That's exactly what I want. "How do you do that?" I ask him. "Can you read my mind?"

He laughs. "It's what you got last time. Now go. You're

hopping from one foot to the other, and there might be a line for the washroom."

In the bathroom stall, I sit with my elbows on my knees, my chin in my hands and heave an enormous sigh. Cameron and I have stopped sniping at each other. He's being a perfect gentleman, and he's keeping his hands off me. I should be happy.

I'm not happy. Every nice thing Cameron does reminds me how much we used to love each other. When he gave me the car keys, my insides fluttered. When he remembered my burger order, my knees grew weak.

You still have feelings for him.

I quell that wayward thought. It's been a long time since I was with a man. Maybe the reason I'm drawn to Cameron is sexual chemistry, nothing else.

Of course, I'm fooling myself. If this was just about physical attraction, my heart wouldn't have melted when he offered to help me buy the right clothes to wear to his family vacation. If this was just lust, I wouldn't have been touched that he remembered the way I took my coffee.

One month, I tell myself firmly. *This is a business deal. Don't embarrass yourself by mooning over Cameron.*

Nine years ago, he didn't care enough to come for me. Why would things be different now?

WHEN WE FINALLY REACH THE cottage, there's a handful of cars parked among the trees. "Everyone's here, I see," Cameron says, his voice as bleak as a cold and rainy day. "Ready to go face the family, Mads?"

Cameron will take a very dim view if I throw up in his car. I take a deep, steadying breath. "As ready as I'll ever be," I lie.

"Hey." His voice softens. "This won't be hard, I promise. No one will have any reason to doubt our relationship. Everyone here knows I was crazy about you." He takes my hand in his, turns it and kisses my palm gently. "I want the cottage," he says. "But I'm not going to throw you to the wolves, Maddie."

Everyone knows I was crazy about you.

As we get out, the front door opens and a man with salt-and-pepper hair comes out, an older version of the man at my side. My stomach plummets. I'd hoped to be able to settle in before being forced to deal with Joseph Drake, but that's not to be.

"Hello father," Cameron greets the man coolly. "You remember Maddie, don't you?"

Cameron's father is shocked at my reappearance in his son's life. He recoils instinctively, before collecting himself. "How can I forget Maddie?" he replies coldly, shaking my hand briefly before dropping it as if I'm carrying a contagious virus. "You're late. I thought you'd be here for lunch."

Ignoring the rebuke, Cameron pops the trunk open and gets our luggage. "Where's everyone?" he asks.

"On the dock," he replies. "Cameron, you need to say hello to your family. I'm sure Maddie will excuse you for an hour."

"The greetings will keep." Cameron laces his hand in mine. "Maddie and I are going to get settled in, unpack and find a cold beer first."

Warmth fills me at Cameron's gesture of support. But when I meet Joseph Drake's icy glare, I suppress a shiver. Nine years ago, Cameron's dad hated the sight of me, and nothing's changed in the intervening years.

I will never belong here, and I can't allow myself to forget that.

"Hey," Cameron nudges me with his shoulder as his father disappears from view. "You okay?"

No, I'm not okay. I'm thrown back to the past. I'm in the bedroom I'm sharing with Cameron, dressed in a cheap polyester dress, and Joseph Drake is eying me with barely concealed contempt. *Your mother's a junkie, and your father is a two-bit crook who's serving his second jail term,* he sneers. *It's obvious you're with my son for his money.*

"What does it matter?" I reply bitterly. "This is a business deal between us, Cam. I pretend to be your fiancée for five hundred thousand dollars. Let's not make this something it isn't, shall we?"

I tell myself that I don't care about the way Cameron stiffens and draws away from me, a shuttered look on his face. I tell myself that he's just pretending to give a damn about me to get what he wants.

But there's a sinking feeling in my heart that tells me I'm wrong, and I can't shake off the sense that I've damaged something between us.

7

CAMERON

"What are you doing with her?" my father puts his hand on my bicep and tugs me to a halt just as I'm making my way down the stairs to the kitchen. Maddie's in the shower, and the thought of her, naked and soapy, fills me with a frustrated heat.

This is just business. I can't let Maddie Morland break my heart again.

My father continues his tirade. "Have you forgotten that she's only interested in you for your money?"

I give his hand a pointed glare until he removes it. Joseph Drake was an indifferent parent who was never around when I was growing up. I was raised by nannies. When I was eight, I remember being terrified that I'd pass my father on the street and not recognize him, I'd seen him so rarely.

Then there were the affairs, a string of mistresses hidden away from my mother, until one ugly day when the entire truth came out and my mother left him.

"Madison is my fiancée," I say through clenched teeth.

"You *will* be polite to her, and you *will* treat her with all the respect she deserves."

"You're a fool," he snaps back. "Sleep with this woman. Set her up in an apartment, give her expensive gifts. But you are a Drake. You don't marry her kind."

"What kind is that?" If my father has any sense, he'd hear the warning in my voice and take heed. Yes, Maddie's family is far from perfect, but I've known that since the moment I met her. It's never mattered to me. It isn't as if my family is free of sin. My grandfather's father amassed his fortune by lying, cheating, and with deceit. When a poor man cheats, he's considered a swindler and tossed in jail. When a billionaire does it, it's just good business.

He subsides, but from the set of his jaw, I know we aren't done with this topic.

In the large eat-in kitchen, Aunt Emily greets the two of us with obvious excitement. "Maddie," she exclaims, her lined face lighting up with joy. "I didn't know you and Cameron were dating again." Her eyes drop to Maddie's left hand, and she squeaks in glee. "You two are engaged? Why, that's wonderful. Isn't it, dad?"

My grandfather, who is seated at the table, reading the newspaper, gives me a sharp look, one that I meet with a bland smile. "You remember Maddie, don't you, grandfather?"

"Yes, of course." Edward Drake rises to his feet and extends his hand in Maddie's direction, and she shakes it, her expression neutral. "Pardon my surprise. Cameron's kept you rather quiet--I had no idea you two were seeing each other." He pastes a polite smile on his face. "It's a pleasure to have you with us this week."

"Thank you," Maddie replies.

My grandfather introduces Maddie to his friends, Bob and Patti Stevens, an older couple that I've met a few times. Once the introductions are done, Maddie bends down to hug my aunt in her wheelchair, her face creasing into a smile. "I've missed you," she says, her voice warm as she addresses my favorite relative. "It's been far too long. What are you reading nowadays?"

The two of them launch into an animated conversation about books. I grab a beer from the refrigerator and join my cousin Noah, who's sitting in a corner of the room, staring moodily out of the window. "What's eating you?"

He shrugs. "It's a long story," he replies. "So, she's the one that got away? I don't blame her for running from this crowd." He gives my grandfather and my father a disgusted look. "If you care about this girl, why on earth have you dragged her into this den of vipers?"

I watch Maddie and my aunt chat amicably, their heads bent toward each other. Maddie is the only person I've met who treats my aunt like a normal person. Everyone else coddles Aunt Emily because she's paralyzed from the waist down, or they talk to her in slow, clear syllables, as if she lost the ability to communicate when she lost her ability to move. Not my Maddie.

As if she senses my gaze on her, Maddie lifts her head up and smiles widely at me. "Sorry Cam," she says with a rueful laugh. "But you don't read sci-fi, and neither does Misti. You have no idea how nice it is to be able to talk about the same books."

I grin back at her, aware that the entire room is covertly watching us while pretending to do something else. "I'll share you for a bit," I tell her. "But only because it's Aunt Emily."

My grandfather chuckles. My dad bares his teeth in a smile that looks more like a snarl. Maddie blushes faintly, and I want to fold her into my arms.

This entire pretense is so you can buy the cottage, I remind myself.

Except I'm lying.

The truth is, I'm falling in love with Maddie all over again. My heart has stayed in stasis all these years, only to come back to life in Maddie's presence.

And she has the power to break it into a million jagged pieces.

I can't allow myself to be vulnerable. Maddie has made it clear that this is a business deal. Once the month is up, she'll take her five hundred thousand dollars and head back to Calgary, and I'll be left without her once again.

"That went okay, don't you think?" Upstairs after dinner, in the privacy of our bedroom, Maddie gives me a questioning look. "You think people bought that we're engaged?"

"Yes." I keep my reply short.

Her phone beeps. She smiles as she reads the contents of her screen. "Misti loved her flight," she says, holding her phone toward me. "She had her first glass of champagne."

I ignore the outstretched phone. "That's good, Maddie."

She notices my one-word answers. "Is everything alright, Cam?" she asks hesitantly.

I have to protect myself, Mads. Because I feel too much around you and I don't know what I'm going to do when you leave me again.

"Sure." I lift my shoulder in a dismissive shrug. "We're alone. No need to act anymore, right?"

A flash of hurt crosses her face. I feel like a heel at her

expression. "Fair enough," she says stiffly. "Do you need the bathroom before I shower?"

As she speaks, she clenches her eyes shut and rubs at her temples with a frown. Her forehead is furrowed and she's paler than she was during the day.

When we dated, Maddie used to get really bad stress migraines. I cross over and dim the light. "Headache?" I ask her.

She nods miserably. "I felt it come on during dinner," she confesses. "Only your family would have a three course sit down meal at a cottage. I didn't want to embarrass you by using the wrong fork."

"You think I care about shit like that?"

She shakes her head. "No," she whispers. "You never treated me like I didn't belong."

My heart feels like it's being squeezed by a powerful fist. "Come here," I tell her gruffly, sitting on the bed, my back against the headboard and patting my thigh. "Does a scalp massage still help?"

"Yes." She sinks down on the mattress and places her head on my lap. I stroke her hair, softly, soothingly. "Close your eyes, baby."

Her eyes are green pools of gratitude. "Thank you, Cam," she murmurs.

"Shh..." With any luck, after a hot shower, some herbal tea and a good night's sleep, Maddie will be as right as rain. I peck out a one-handed text to Noah telling him to put the kettle on, and continue rubbing gently at her scalp until Maddie dozes off.

Ten minutes later, there's a soft tap at the door. I move a pillow under Maddie's head and slide to my feet.

Noah holds a tray up at me. There's a teapot there as well as a selection of teas and milk, sugar, honey and lemon.

"I didn't know how Maddie takes her tea," he explains. "Is she okay?"

"It's a migraine. She gets them when she's stressed." Taking the tray from him, I set it down at the side of the bed. Maddie stirs, but doesn't wake. I shut the door and join Noah on the landing. "She's usually fine after a good night's sleep."

"You shouldn't have brought her here." Noah's voice holds an edge of condemnation. "Aunt Emily was right to be concerned."

That catches my attention. "What did she say?"

"Something about your father driving her away the first time," he replies. "What the heck were you thinking, Cameron?"

"I would never hurt her deliberately." I cling to those words as self-defense.

Noah gives me a scornful look. "I hope that helps you sleep tonight."

As tempting as it would be to lash out at my cousin, I know he's right. I should have found some other way to get my grandfather to sell me the cottage. Now, a woman I care about deeply is in pain because of my machinations.

I hear movement inside the room. "I have to check up on her," I tell my cousin, already turning the handle of the door. I can't help feeling like I've fucked up again. It's up to me now to make amends, as best as I can.

Maddie's sitting up, leaning against the headboard, her eyes clenched shut. "Cam?"

"How's the head?" Without waiting for her to reply, I tear open a chamomile tea bag and pour some hot water into it, stirring in a generous spoonful of honey. "Here. Drink."

She sips obediently from the cup I hold to her lips. "You

remember the way I like my tea," she says softly. "You remembered my burger order, too."

I tuck a stray curl behind her ear. "Did you think I could forget you, Mads?"

"You didn't call me." Her voice catches on the words. "I left and you never called."

I stare at her, even though her eyes are shut and she can't see my expression. "Did you expect me to?" I can't completely conceal the hurt from my tone. My father offered her money to leave me, and she took it. Hopped in a cab and exited my life. Did she expect me to chase after her?

She heaves a sigh. "Never mind. We agreed not to talk about the past."

I'm an idiot. I've already caused her stress tonight. Now I'm fighting about something that happened nine years ago. "Do you want me to run a bath for you?" I trace the line of her jaw with my finger and she shivers in response, and my body responds, as always, to her.

She's sick, Cameron. This isn't the time...

I turn the hot water tap on in the tub and help her to the bathroom. "Stay," she whispers, as I turn to leave. "Keep me company, Cam?"

Maddie's always been strong. It kills me to see her so weakened, so frail. "Whatever you want, baby." I turn my head away as she strips out of the dress she wore to dinner, and I mutter curses and do multiplication tables under my breath as she removes her bra and panties. She's so beautiful. Her large breasts were made for my touch, my tongue. Her pink-tipped nipples are swollen, and as she steps into the tub, I catch a glimpse of her pussy.

Trying to distract myself from the sight of her naked body, I fiddle with my phone and find some soothing music to play.

When she's ready to get out, I towel her dry and guide her to the bed, and tuck the blankets around her. I'm about to make a bed for myself on the floor when she makes a soft protest. "Will you hold me, Cam?"

I've never been able to say no to her. I've never wanted to. I climb into bed and wrap my arms around her. "I'd do anything for you, sweetheart," I whisper into her hair. She doesn't hear me. Safe in my arms, she's fallen fast asleep.

And I'm left with a stark realization. It's too late for me. It was always too late. I should have known it the instant I saw her at the funeral home.

Once again, I've fallen in love with Madison Morland.

8

MADDIE

I wake up slowly. I'm wrapped in someone's arms, my head resting on someone's shoulder.

Cameron's arms. Cameron's shoulder.

In his sleep, he looks relaxed, peaceful. Memories from last night slowly come creeping back. His father had glared at me all the way through dinner. His grandfather had barely spoken. Noah had been obviously bitter and angry about something.

Emily had done her best to ignore the stress in the room and carry on a conversation with me, but it hadn't been enough. Halfway through dinner, dots of light started appearing in my vision, and I knew that a migraine was inevitable.

Cameron had taken such good care of me. His fingers had massaged my scalp until the blinding pain had receded. He'd poured me some tea and run me a bath, and when I got out of the steaming water, he'd toweled me dry.

Admit it, Maddie. You have feelings for this guy.

At the risk of sounding like a cliché, it's always been Cam for me. There's a reason I found it hard to date in Calgary, a reason I gave Jenna the business card of one of the richest men in Western Canada without a second thought.

You told him the only reason you're here is for the money.

I bite my lip and stifle my sigh. It shouldn't matter what Cameron thinks about me, but it does. I don't want him to think that I'm interested in him for his money. His wealth has never mattered. Had it not been for my desperate need to make sure that Misti's future is brighter than mine, I wouldn't have accepted his offer.

Then tell him the truth, my conscience urges. *Tell him why you wanted the cash. He deserves to know.*

Cameron stirs, and a different memory jolts me awake. I didn't want my pajamas last night. I'm naked, pressed against Cameron's body. And he's wearing a pair of boxers and nothing else.

Well, hello, morning wood.

My throat is dry. I'm having a hard time remembering the many good reasons I should resist Cameron's sexual magnetism. I should disentangle myself, get up, get dressed, put some distance between us...

I stay exactly where I am, luxuriating in the blatantly masculine allure of his body. My eyes wander, feasting on his hard chest, on the six pack abs, on the tempting bulge that's tenting his boxers.

"See anything you like?"

My eyes fly to his face. There's a glimmer of amusement in his eyes, and a hunger that he doesn't try to conceal.

It takes less than a second to make my decision. "Maybe," I reply, my tone coy. "If you take off your boxers, I'll be able to decide."

He pushes me on my back and moves over me, a knee between my thighs, his weight resting on his hands on either side of me. His blue eyes bore into mine. "If I take off my boxers, I'm going to fuck you."

I feel a rush of wetness in my pussy from his firm tone. "What are you waiting for?" I ask, my voice almost trembling with need. I reach for the waistband of his shorts, intent on getting rid of the offending garment.

He stops me with a shake of his head. "I don't think so, Mads. I've waited for you too long to rush this. Put your hands behind your head."

"Cam," I pout. Knowing Cameron, he'll keep me at the edge of orgasm for hours, reducing me to a trembling, quivering mess before he gives me what I want.

"Maddie." He smirks at me, knowing I'm going to obey. "Would you prefer to be tied up?"

Yes. Yes, please.

I move my hands behind my head. "So bossy," I complain.

"And you love it, baby."

He kisses me, deep and long, one hand cupping my breast. His thumb grazes my nipple and I moan into his mouth. "Harder," I beg. It takes all the control I possess to keep from reaching up and pulling him closer to me, to refrain from running my fingers through his dark hair.

"So bossy," he rumbles, echoing my words. "You need to learn patience, Maddie."

His thumb swipes over my nipple again, then he rubs it between his thumb and forefinger. Heated pleasure spirals through me. "Fuck patience," I say through clenched teeth. "Do that again."

He chuckles and repeats the motion and I whimper, writhing under his body. "Cam," I beg.

"Yes, Maddie?" His teeth flash in a grin, then he pushes

my breasts together, and nips them, each bite sending a sharp pinch of lust through me.

My pussy drips with every bite and I squirm restlessly, spreading my legs open, hoping he'll get the hint. "Cameron," I say warningly. "Stop teasing me. I want you now."

"Tsk, tsk." He chuckles as he takes in my frustrated expression. "I thought you liked foreplay, Maddie." He rains kisses over my body as he speaks, my neck, my throat, my erect nipples. With each kiss, his stubble scratches my skin, generating more heat, until I'm half-crazed with lust and desperate for more.

"There's a time for foreplay," I complain plaintively. "This isn't it."

He slides down my body, sending delicious friction sparkling through every nerve ending. "Spread your legs for me, Maddie," he orders. His hands hold my thighs open and his tongue trails a slow path down my pussy. My breath catches. "Ah," he groans, his fingers gripping my flesh, "the way you taste…"

I flush scarlet, but the embarrassment is quickly overtaken by heat. Cameron feasts on me as if he were a starving man at an all-you-can-eat buffet, his tongue circling my clitoris, his fingers pumping in and out of my pussy. I grip the pillowcase under my head and whimper for more.

Okay, I change my mind about foreplay. He can do this all day.

"You like this, don't you, Maddie?" His words come out muffled. His thumb presses down on my bundle of nerves, and his tongue probes at my entrance, and I explode. My orgasm thunders through me, intense, overwhelming. I cling on to Cameron, my hands fisting in his hair, and I drown in wave after wave of heat and desire and pleasure.

He climbs off the bed and undresses, and his erection springs free. My mouth goes dry. I've forgotten how large Cameron is. I watch him with hungry eyes as he takes a condom out of his wallet and rolls it on. "Come here," I whisper. "I want to touch you."

His eyebrows rise. "Did you move your hands, baby?" His voice is silky.

I grin at him, wide, filled with pure happiness. "I did. Are you going to spank me for being bad?"

He laughs and lowers himself between my legs. "Later," he says. His head nudges inside and I stop breathing, my entire body going still as I wait for his length to slide inside me. "Right now," he murmurs, "I'm far too busy enjoying the way you feel."

He thrusts his hips forward and enters me all the way. I groan as his thick shaft fills me completely. "Cameron," I whisper, wrapping my hands around his neck and kissing him. "Please..."

"Please do this?" His voice is strained, his customary amusement absent, replaced by intensity. He withdraws from me, before slamming back into my pussy.

"Yes," I sob as every nerve ending in my body comes alive. "Yes, please. More..."

He cups my breast and bends his head, licking and sucking at my nipple. I arch toward him, willing him to move faster.

He just grins down at me. "You're in such a hurry, baby. What's the rush?"

"Cameron," I hiss out, clenching the muscles in my pussy around his cock. From his sharp intake of breath, I know he can feel me. *Time to up the ante.* I move my right hand toward my pussy. "Are you going to fuck me or do I have to pleasure myself?"

Heat blazes in his eyes. "You like to live on the edge, don't you, baby?" Cam says, his tone smooth, sexy and oh-so-controlled. His palm comes into sharp contact against my ass. "Moving your hands without permission, sassing me, ordering me around." His hand moves my wrists back into position as he flexes in me. "If you want to come again," he says, "I suggest you start doing as you're told."

I have no desire to be controlled outside the bedroom. But here? When Cameron talks to me in that tone, telling me that I'll obey *or else,* my pussy gushes in response, my nipples pebble and I want him more than ever.

Plus, I like it when he spanks me. *I like it a lot.*

And a perverse part of me wonders if he'll spank me harder if I sass him more. "Shut up and fuck me," I tell him, tightening my pussy once again.

He pushes my legs in the air. "Hold yourself open," he orders, and I obediently lace my hands around my thighs, my knees doubling back over my shoulders. "You want to be fucked deep, baby? Well, you're going to get fucked deep. Hang on."

I hang on. He slams into me, hard, fast, and I feel him deep in my gut. He's buried so deep. His balls slap against my ass as he thrusts, over and over again, his breathing harsh and uneven.

With each stroke, my insides tighten. Desire threatens to overflow as he pistons in and out, his palm spanking my exposed ass as he fucks me. "Such a bad girl," he pants out. "Is this what you want, Maddie? You want to be taken hard? You want to be spanked until you come?"

"Yes," I shout out, forgetting completely that someone is in the bedroom next to us. "Yes, please. Cam." I can't hold it back anymore. I want to prolong this orgasm, but I can't. It's too much. I'm coming apart with pleasure, my core suffused with red hot heat. "I'm coming," I gasp out, my voice shaking, my entire body trembling.

His hands grip my thighs. "Fuck," he says through clenched teeth. His forehead is furrowed. Lines of need are etched into his face. He redoubles the intensity of his thrusts, faster, harder, until he comes with a loud groan.

He slumps on top of me, sated. I wrap my arms around his waist and hold him.

Whatever happens between us, I never want to forget this moment. In this moment, there is nothing other than truth between us. We can't lie about our need. We can't pretend we don't want each other.

"I PROBABLY SHOULD HAVE ASKED you how your headache was before I jumped you."

I stretch languidly, long-unused muscles protesting in response. "I think I jumped you, not the other way around."

He pulls me into his arms with a smile. "Okay," he says agreeably. "If you jumped me, you'll have to let me even the score."

More sex with Cameron? I know our relationship is fake, and I know that things are going to end after a month. Yet, I'm on board. Call me crazy, but either way, I'm going to get my heart broken. This way, at least I'll have a month of amazing sex first. "Sounds good," I reply, burrowing myself against him.

My conscience chooses this moment to intervene with an inconvenient reminder. *You promised yourself you'd tell him the truth about the money.*

"Cameron? There's something I want to tell you."

His lips press a soft kiss against my hair. "You want the bathroom first?" he asks, his voice teasing.

If only it were that simple. "No, that's not it. I need to tell you about the money."

He stiffens at my side. "What money?" he asks, his voice wary.

I take a deep breath and the words tumble out. Telling the truth is good for the soul, right? It better be. "The reason I agreed to our deal was because Misti lost her college scholarship."

He turns on his side and props himself up by his elbow. "What are you talking about, Maddie?"

"You offered me five hundred thousand dollars to pretend to be engaged to you." Cameron's not usually obtuse. "I wouldn't have done it if Misti hadn't needed the money for college." I give him an appealing look, hoping he'll understand. "I want her to graduate from university, Cam. I want her to have better options than I did."

His gaze softens. "You take good care of her," he says. "Who takes care of you?"

You do, I want to reply, thinking of the way he looked after me last night. But I can't rely on Cameron. Our time together is temporary. "I'm a grown-up," I tell him stoutly. "I can take care of myself."

But as I lie in his arms, I'm not sure if I can. It feels a little too good to be held by him. Sleeping with Cameron is dangerous for my heart.

9

CAMERON

My father's theory about Maddie is that she's a gold-digger, only interested in me for my money.

I've never fully embraced his viewpoint. Only once in my life did I believe his words, and that was in the immediate aftermath of her departure from the cottage. And even then, my hurt had more to do with the fact that she left without a word of explanation, than my father's gloating revelation that she accepted fifty thousand dollars from him to stay away from me. Maddie isn't a mercenary person. If she needed the money to protect her sister and move away from her abusive family, I'm *almost* glad she took it.

This morning, holding Maddie again, kissing her soft lips, sliding into her hot, eager body, I realize that I don't care about the past. Yes, there's a small part of me that wishes that she would explain her side of the events that surrounded her departure from the cottage, but mostly, I'm just glad she's here with me.

"We should get ready." Maddie rolls over and looks at the clock next to the bed, reluctance etched on her face.

"Your grandfather would probably disapprove if we're late for breakfast."

I trace the curve of her hip with my finger. "Screw my grandfather. It's been nine years. Breakfast is the last thing on my mind."

She's tempted, I know, but she shakes her head and pulls away from my grasp. "You want to buy the cottage, remember?" she says. "For Aunt Emily? Well, if that's going to work, we'll need to make a good impression."

"Okay." I stretch on the bed, and the sheet covering my dick slides off. Maddie's eyes immediately move to my cock, which is stirring again. "One more round before we get up?" I ask.

"Cam," she scolds. "We don't have time." She starts walking toward the bathroom, giving me a wicked grin over her shoulder. "Join me in the shower?"

That sounds pretty damn good. "Do you want your back soaped, Maddie?" I ask as I follow her to the en suite. My grandfather has spared no expense here--the walls of the shower stall are embedded with Jacuzzi jets. I turn the water on and watch steam fill the space. My cock hardens as I imagine pressing her round, firm ass against me, sliding a finger inside her and making her come over and over again.

"Yes." She steps into the shower and groans in pleasure as the streams of hot water massage her body. "God, this shower is amazing. You should get this installed at your place."

"Are you offering to visit me if I do?" I enter after her and pull the glass door shut.

"Oh." She flushes. "That wasn't a hint."

"No, you're not the type that hints," I tell her easily, wrapping my arms around her waist and pulling her toward me, her back against my chest. "You've always been pretty direct."

She relaxes against me with a sigh. "Is that a compliment or an insult?" she asks dryly.

I smile and kiss her neck. "It's definitely a compliment, Mads. You have no idea how refreshing it is to be with someone that doesn't play games." I move my hands to caress her breasts. "Talking about games, let's play one."

Her breath catches as I rub her nipple between my thumb and forefinger. "What kind of game?"

"Pick a number between one and ten," I reply.

She shivers as my fingers trail down her flat belly to her mound. I play with her, teasing the crease between her lips, avoiding her clitoris for the moment. "Five," she gasps out.

I bite back my grin. She's not a gambler, my Maddie. Her choice is smack dab in the middle, but it'll do for my purposes. "Good number," I tell her. I unhitch the handheld showerhead from the wall. "Five orgasms it will be."

She turns around to see what I'm doing, and inhales sharply when she catches sight of what I'm holding. "Are you going to do what I think you are?" she asks. There's a mixture of nervousness and anticipation in her tone.

"I am." I nudge her thighs open with my knee. "Turn around and lean against me, and wrap your arms around my neck. And keep those legs spread, honey."

She obeys with a nervous chuckle, her skin soft against mine. "You're crazy, you know that? We're going to be late for breakfast."

"We have plenty of time." I adjust the nozzle and part her folds with the fingers of one hand. "Ready, baby? Here we go."

The jet of water hits her pussy and she rises on tiptoe to meet it. "Oh my God," she sobs out, pressing into me harder, her nails digging into the back of my neck. She moves and writhes, her face contorted with pleasure. She's at the edge in less than two minutes. "I'm coming," she groans as her body tightens in climax.

"That's one."

She half-chuckles, half-moans. "You're an evil man, Cameron Drake." She squirms as the stream of water hits her puffy, swollen clitoris, dancing around to try and avoid the spray. "Cam, it's too much," she gasps.

"Want me to stop?"

"No," she chokes out. "Not yet." That's my Maddie. She might not be a gambler, but she also won't back down. A fact I'm taking full advantage of at the moment.

Her pants and her moans, her ass rubbing into my dick, her soft cries of pleasure have me ready to burst. She comes a second time, then a third and a fourth, but before she can come one final time, I drop the shower-head and twist her toward me, rolling a condom on my dick.

Her eyes open wide. "You brought a condom into the shower?"

I'm too far gone for conversation. "I used to be a boy scout," I grind out as I lift her up and lower her on my cock, moving us until her back is pressed against the wall. "This is going to be hard and fast, baby, with an emphasis on fast." I've watched her come four fucking times. I'm not going to last much longer.

She isn't listening. She's making mewling sounds as I slam her down on my cock. She's so tight. Her pussy is swollen after her orgasms, and each time I bounce her on me, she whimpers. "Touch yourself," I order. "Come with me."

Her hazel eyes are clouded with need. She moves her hand between our bodies, down to her pussy. She starts rubbing herself, her entire body trembling. Her muscles clench around my cock, and her fingers graze against my shaft as I thrust in and out of her.

"Fuck," she wails, on the verge of her climax. "Cam, I can't hold on..."

My thrusts aren't controlled anymore. I see spots in front of me as I move faster and faster. The water still drenches our bodies, and steam fills the shower stall. I don't notice. All that matters are the tremors that run through her pussy. My world narrows, my body stiffens and, just as her climax overtakes her, I erupt.

As we make our way downstairs for breakfast, I look out of the window and grimace. It's raining outside, and we're going to be stuck indoors all day. Great. I'd hoped to spend as little time as possible with my family, but the weather has found a way to thwart me.

It gets worse. We reach the dining room and I come to a stop at the doorway. Sitting at the table are the two people that are responsible for my entire ruse. My cousin Ryder is sipping a cup of coffee and is saying something to my grandfather, one arm possessively draped around the shoulders of his wife, Zoe.

Fuck.

"Ah, there you are." My grandfather smiles at Maddie with more warmth than he's shown so far. "Did you sleep well, my dear? Noah tells me you had a migraine last night."

"I did, thank you." She squeezes my hand and takes a seat at the large dining table. "Cameron took very good care of me."

My grandfather gives me a searching gaze. "I'm glad to

hear it," he says. "It's time he settled down and took his responsibilities seriously."

I ignore the implied rebuke and reach across the table to shake Ryder's hand. I don't know my cousin and his wife very well, but Ryder seems like a decent guy, very unlike his father, who had been the family black sheep. "I hear congratulations are in order," I tell them.

"Thanks, Cameron." Zoe smiles widely at me. "And this must be your fiancée." She turns to Maddie. "Hi, I'm Zoe."

The two of them exchange handshakes. "Pity about the weather," Zoe sighs, looking at the rain. "I was hoping to spend some time on the dock working on my tan. Still, there's always tomorrow, right?"

I think rapidly. Ryder being here has complicated things. When my grandfather talked about selling the cottage, I assumed I had some time to change his mind, but it appears that things are moving faster than I anticipated. "Are you guys here for the weekend?"

Sure enough, Ryder confirms my hunch with his next words. "No, Zoe persuaded me to take some time off. We're here all week."

Zoe snorts. "I think Ryder means to say that I threw a tantrum," she says frankly. "Is Cam a workaholic too?" she asks Maddie. "You have no idea how hard it is to get Ryder to take a vacation."

"Hey," Ryder protests, giving his wife a fond look. "Let's change the topic from my many failings, shall we? Cameron, nice car, buddy."

We pass the time in idle conversation while we wait for Noah, Aunt Emily, and my father to join us at breakfast. After the meal, Zoe pulls a game of Pictionary from a bookshelf. "I haven't played this in years," she exclaims. "Shall we?"

My father immediately excuses himself and leaves the room. My grandfather declines to play as well, but settles himself on an armchair in the living room with a book. That leaves six of us. "I won't be any use," Aunt Emily protests, her face distressed. "I can't draw."

"You don't have to, Emily," Maddie says, squeezing my aunt's shoulder. "You can guess though, right?" She smiles persuasively at my aunt. "Come on. It'll be fun."

We draw up teams. Maddie, Emily and I are in one; Ryder, Zoe and Noah are on the other.

The game gets underway. Ryder, being an architect, is very good at sketching, so their team solves the first clue and takes the lead. Then it's our turn. "Which one of you is drawing?" Noah asks.

"Maddie," I announce with a smirk.

She groans. "I can't draw for peanuts," she says. "We're going to get killed."

Ryder looks up. "Really?" he drawls, a gleam in his eyes. "How about we make this interesting? Cam, a wager?"

I quirk an eyebrow. "What's at stake?"

"We win and you let all of us drive your car."

Zoe laughs out loud. "I wouldn't let Ryder attend the classic car auction," she confesses. "He's been pouting ever since he found out you bought the Carrera." She shudders in mock horror. "You drive it," she says to Ryder. "I'm not going to. That car is a little too rich for me. A million dollars, right, Cameron? I'd be terrified of wrecking it."

My grandfather speaks up from his corner. "I doubt Cameron's going to take this wager," he says. "From what I hear, he doesn't let anyone drive his car."

Maddie looks up, surprised. "That's not true. He let me drive it here."

"Really?" My grandfather gives me another long, considering look. "Is that so?"

I kiss Maddie's cheek. "You're not anyone, baby," I say to her. "You're my fiancée. What's mine is yours. Of course you can drive the Porsche." To Ryder, I nod. "Alright, you're on. And if you lose?"

He shrugs. "I'm sure you'll think of something."

Good. That's exactly what I hoped he'd say. Ryder's a decent enough guy. I think he'll walk away from this cottage deal if he knows why I want it, but even so, a little extra help will come in handy.

Maddie draws a card and frowns when she reads the clue. "Ready?" Noah asks her, his hand on the little plastic sand hourglass. She thinks for a second, then nods.

She draws some squiggly lines, then adds a stick figure in the middle. "Swimming," I guess. She beams at me and starts drawing more stick figures. One with its arm raised in the air, another with it extending forward. "A kind of stroke? Freestyle?"

"Yes." She throws her pad in the air in jubilation. "Cam, you're my hero."

"Come on." Noah rolls his eyes. "You guys met during a swim-meet, didn't you? That's not even a challenge."

I roll the dice. Six. Yes. Advancing our token, I smirk at the other team. "Game on."

It's a close game. Ryder can draw, but Zoe can't and neither can Noah. Though Maddie likes to claim she can't draw a straight line with the help of a ruler, she's pretty good at getting her meaning across.

Both teams draw for the final turn. Zoe and I read the clue, and I chuckle. *Bacon.* I've got this.

I draw a woman with a ring on her finger. "Me?" Maddie guesses, her eyebrow raised. I nod. *Smart girl.*

Across from me, Zoe's trying to draw a pig, but it looks like a blob with four legs. Ryder's forehead scrunches with puzzlement. "Cat? Dog?"

I quickly sketch a table with a plate on it. "A meal?" Maddie asks. "A meal for me? Something I like to eat? Bacon?"

"Yes." I punch my fist in the air and kiss Maddie soundly on the lips. "I love you, Mads."

Ryder and Noah are too busy laughing at Zoe's pig to pay attention to us. But Aunt Emily is right next to us, and she hears what I said, as does my grandfather, watching intently from his corner.

I don't have eyes for them. I'm watching Maddie.

She goes still as she registers the words, then her expression closes. Pasting a polite smile on her face, she rises to her feet, refusing to meet my eyes. "Will you excuse me?" she says stiffly. "I need to get a coffee refill."

That's not the reaction I'd hoped for. Not at all.

10

MADDIE

I love you, Mads.

I make my way to the kitchen with unseeing eyes. The housekeeper, Mrs. Coleman is there, wiping down a counter. "Can I help you, Ms. Morland?" she asks me with a pleasant smile.

"I just want some more coffee."

I love you, Mads. How many times have I dreamed of hearing those words in the last nine years? How many times have I fantasized about Cameron finding me, coming to Calgary, saying those words to me, whispering that he can't live without me?

So many times. And now he's said those words to me, and it's not even remotely like the fantasies. Because it's all fake. Ryder and Zoe were in the room, obviously in love with each other, and Cameron wants to buy the cottage.

Get a grip on yourself, I order. *You knew what was involved this week. You agreed to play along.*

I hear footsteps. I'm half-expecting Cam to follow me, but it's Zoe that enters the room. Of course. Cameron doesn't follow me when I run away. I should have learned that lesson nine years ago, when I waited for him to call, email me, anything to show me he cared.

Zoe must see some of my distress in my face. "Maddie?" she asks softly. "Is everything okay?"

I lift my shoulders in a shrug, aware that Mrs. Coleman is within earshot. "I just needed caffeine."

"Sure." Her expression says she doesn't believe a word. "Let's take a walk, shall we?"

I glance at the window. The rain's softened into a drizzle, and the sun is shining from a gap in the clouds. "You're going to get wet."

She snorts. "I'm not made of sugar, Maddie. Despite what Ryder thinks, I won't melt." She makes her way to the cloakroom and I follow her. She puts on a raincoat and I pick up an umbrella, and we make our way outside.

"This place is crazy, isn't it?" she continues conversationally as we walk down the tree-lined path toward the dock. "I mean, who has a housekeeper for a cottage?"

"You find it strange? I thought you'd be used to it."

"Because of Ryder?" She shakes her head. "No, I didn't grow up with this kind of wealth. We're dirt poor."

"Really?" I can't hide the surprise from my voice. "You seem to fit in really well." *In a way I've never been able to.*

"They're just people, Maddie," she replies with a roll of her eyes. "If you scratch them, they will bleed. If you hurt them, they will ache."

"They eat fried chicken with a knife and fork," I blurt out.

"Huh?" Zoe shoots me a puzzled look.

"The last time I was here," I explain, "we had a picnic on the lawn. They had fried chicken, coleslaw, potato salad, all kinds of picnic food. I thought I knew how to behave at a picnic, so I flopped down on a blanket with a chicken leg." I frown at the humiliating memory. "And Cameron's dad looked down at me, and he asked me, loud enough for everyone to hear, *'what on earth are you doing?'*"

Even now, I can't forget the sinking feeling in my stomach as I realized that the entire party had turned to look at me.

Zoe squeezes my hand in sympathy. "That's awful. What did you do?"

What happened next is my favorite part of this memory. "I was too shocked to respond, but Cam heard his dad. He came and sat next to me with a leg of chicken in his hand, and he proceeded to eat it with his fingers, as if that's what everyone was expected to do."

At that time, I'd been too mortified to register Cameron's support. Now, I think back and realize that Cameron had, without the slightest bit of hesitation, picked a side that day. He came and sat by me on the blanket, rather than sit with his family at the picnic table.

That day. Two days later, he'd changed his mind. When I'd left the cottage, he'd stayed behind, and let our relationship wither on the vine.

"He loves you very much," Zoe says softly.

He wants the cottage, I think sadly, trying to ignore the leap in my heart at Zoe's words. Cam doesn't love me--he's just pretending so his grandfather will sell him the cottage.

He took really good care of you last night, and there was no one there to watch.

"Ryder's told me about the two of you," she continues. "You used to date in high school, right? And ever since you left, Cameron's never dated anyone for longer than a month?" She sighs. "And now you're engaged. So romantic. It's like the movies."

I look discomfited and Zoe laughs awkwardly. "Sorry,"

she apologizes. "I swear the pregnancy is making me more emotional. Hormones. I'm not usually this sentimental, really."

I laugh at her earnest expression. I like Zoe. She's friendly and down-to-earth. "I think your husband and my fiancé are looking for us," I tell her, spotting the two men strolling along the path behind us.

"Of course they are." Her lips turn up in a grin as Ryder and Cameron catch up with us. "Hi honey. Are you going to lecture me about catching a cold in the rain?"

"Someone has to be the sensible one." Ryder laces his fingers in hers. "The third time I met Zoe, she was on the roof of her grandmother's house, forty feet off the ground, replacing shingles. And she's terrified of heights."

Cameron's blue eyes search my face. *Are you okay?* he seems to ask me.

My heart hammers in my chest. *He followed me.* I ran out of the living room, convinced he wouldn't follow. I was wrong because here he is, looking at me with concerned eyes.

"Maddie isn't much better," Cameron says, not taking his eyes away from me. "You're carrying an umbrella, but you didn't think to open it? You need someone to take care of you, silly goose."

I get the strangest sense that we're not talking about the rain anymore. *Underneath, we're talking about something else.*

My heart warms at the fondness in his voice. "It wasn't raining that hard," I point out, unable to meet his gaze. What is he saying? Does he want to be with me, or are his words for Ryder and Zoe's benefit?

He came after you. This time around, can things be different?

I'm not sure. But I'm not the same person I was nine

years ago. I recognize Joseph Drake's attempts to intimidate me for what they are.

Cameron's changed, too. He took me shopping and helped me find the right clothes to wear, something he wouldn't have thought of before. He's stuck by me, a solid, supportive presence at my side.

Maybe we're both reaching out, imperfect and tentative from the hurt we've experienced in the past, yet unable to resist the pull we feel.

I put my arm around Cameron's waist. If he stiffens, if he rejects me now…

He doesn't. He takes the umbrella from my nerveless fingers with a crooked smile, opens it and holds it over my head. "Come on Maddie, let's go in."

THREE DAYS LATER, I have to admit I'm having a really good time. Yes, Cameron's dad is still glowering at me, but he's the only one. Cam's grandfather has thawed and Aunt Emily is as warm as ever. Noah is still angry with his grandfather for some reason, but he's friendly with Cam, Ryder, Zoe, and me.

Most importantly, things are pretty great with Cameron. During the days, we swim in the lake and drink beer on the dock. Our nights are spent rekindling the flame between us.

By unspoken mutual agreement, we don't discuss the past, and we don't look ahead to the future. We stay in the present and it's good. Really good.

I should have known it wouldn't last.

Wednesday morning, Misti calls me. "There's a problem."

She sounds distressed. My stomach sinks. "What's the matter?"

"I just got a call from dad. He's being released from prison at the end of the week. And Maddie?" Her voice breaks. "I'm so sorry. He wormed out of me that you were back with Cameron. I think he's going to try to contact you."

Of course he is. My father has always been very aware of exactly how much money Cameron is worth.

Nine years ago, the news that my dad was being released from prison prompted Cameron's father to confront me about the unsuitability of our relationship.

"Cameron could be a senator. He could even be Prime Minister one day." He pauses significantly. *"Unless he's hampered by his wife's family."*

He takes out his checkbook, his eyes hard. "How much money do I have to pay you to get you to walk out of my son's life?"

"What?" I look at him, shocked. I know he doesn't like me, but offering to pay me?

"Your mother's a junkie, and your father is a two-bit crook who's serving his second jail term," he sneers. "It's obvious you're with my son for his money. So, what will it take?"

I can't deal with this. I'm already freaking out about my dad leeching off Cameron's wealth. I don't have the stamina for a confrontation with Joseph Drake now.

The truth is, he's probably right. I can't allow my father to drag Cameron down; I can't let my family tarnish his brightness. When Carl Morland was released from prison, it started a countdown to the end of the best relationship of my life.

I'd written Cameron a letter, tears streaming down my eyes. I'd left it in our bedroom and I'd packed my clothes and called for a cab to take me to the nearest bus stand, and I'd made my way back to Toronto.

All the way home, I'd hoped against hope that he'd call me and tell me we could make it work. *But he'd never called.*

Now, in a sick twist of fate, my dad is getting out of prison again. An urge to flee overwhelms me.

11

CAMERON

"Want to do something different today?" I enter the bedroom, the question on my lips, then come to a halt when I take in Maddie's expression. She's clutching her phone in a death-grip, and her face is pale. "What's wrong?"

She doesn't meet my eyes. "I'll call you back, Misti," she says, and hangs up.

"What's wrong?" I repeat. "Is your sister okay?"

She gives me a small nod and tries to change the subject. "What were you saying? You asked me if I wanted to do something today?"

Damn it, Maddie, talk to me.

She's clearly upset. Her lips tremble as she struggles not to cry, but she's losing the fight. I take one step into the room and fold her into my arms. Her hair smells like summer rain, and her body is soft and warm in my embrace.

I don't talk; I just hold her as she sobs. I rock her back and forth, my hand rubbing her back, soothing her. "Maddie, honey. Please don't cry. Tell me what's wrong so I can fix it."

She half-sobs, half-laughs. "You can't fix everything, you know," she says, her voice muffled into my shoulder. "Sometimes, there are problems even Cameron Drake can't solve."

"Let me be the judge of that."

She laughs this time, a weak and watery laugh, but a laugh nonetheless. "Sorry to fall apart on you," she murmurs, pulling away and reaching for a tissue. "Thanks for letting me cry on your shoulder."

"Anytime, Mads," I say, meaning it.

A fleeting wistful look crosses Maddie's face. "What were you saying when you came in?"

"I thought we could take the boat and head out for the day? Mrs. Coleman can pack us a picnic."

"Just you and me?" she asks hopefully.

I nod. I've enjoyed hanging out with Ryder, Zoe, and Noah, but I want some alone time with Maddie. Sleeping with her every night, spending time with her during the day, I've realized something important. I can't let her go again. I love Maddie.

Nine years ago, I made the biggest mistake of my life. I was devastated that Maddie picked money over me, and I'd allowed bitterness to overtake me.

I was wrong. I should have gone to her, demanded answers. Tried to understand.

I've been given a second chance, and I'm not going to screw it up. Maddie and I are meant to be together.

I toss my phone on the bed. "You and me. No distractions, no interruptions."

Her lips curl into a smile. She drops her phone next to mine. "Sounds amazing."

We head south on Lake Rosseau and thread our way to

Lake Joseph. It's a perfect warm summer day. The water is calm and there's a slight breeze in the air.

At my side, Maddie's quiet, lost in thought. I put my arm around her. "What's bothering you, Mads?"

She sighs. "Why did you want to date me, Cameron? You could have had any girl you wanted."

"Seriously? I was crazy about you."

"Yes, but why?"

"You're really hot," I joke. She digs an elbow in my side. "Okay, okay," I hold up my hands and try to put into words why I'd felt at home with her. "The real reason? I never had to act with you."

She gives me a puzzled look. "Act? Act how?"

"With everyone else, I was Cameron Drake, heir to the Drake billions. My grandfather gave my high school ten million dollars, and they named the library after him. My uncle, Ryder's father, was hockey captain. Every single day, I had to deal with the weight of all those expectations."

I pause to gather my thoughts. "Then I met you. You had no idea who I was, and when you found out, you didn't care. I didn't have to pretend with you." My grip on her hand tightens. "The week I met you, a woman who worked for my father accused him of sexual assault. My grandfather pulled the family together, all of us, and coached us on what to say to the press if we were interviewed." My lips twist into a bitter smile. "Noah was only fourteen. His brothers Zachary and Declan were thirteen. And we were being taught that people only wanted us for our money. When I was with you, I was free of all that bullshit."

She rests her head on my shoulder. "That's horrible," she says quietly. She pauses for a long time. "My father's getting out of prison. That's why I was upset earlier."

Maddie rarely mentions her father. I'm embarrassed to

admit I didn't even know he was in jail. I blink in confusion. "Because he's being released?"

Her mouth curls into a frown. "My father would sell his soul for twenty bucks," she replies. "He's got a drinking problem. He's angry. He's violent. He keeps getting into bar brawls, and he keeps getting arrested for it."

"You weren't close?"

She snorts. "I met him for the first time when I was ten. His kids were never a priority. I was never important. *Until I met you.* Then, suddenly, he was interested in me. It didn't take me long to realize that you were the real target."

I put two and two together. "That's why you're upset? Because your father might extort me?"

She nods. "It's always been the reason," she replies. "Both now and nine years ago. Your dad was concerned that having a father in prison might impact your political career. Me, I was just afraid he'd want money from you."

"What political career?" I absorb the rest of her words and freeze. *When did Maddie and my father have this conversation?* "Say that again."

"I thought we weren't going to rehash the past." She shrugs. "It's okay. You made your choice that day. It's old news now. Water under the bridge."

A cold shiver trickles down my spine. "Humor me," I tell her, my voice clipped. "Tell me exactly what happened."

She gives me a concerned look. "It doesn't matter."

"Tell me," I insist again.

"Fine." She gathers her thoughts. "I was already uncomfortable at the cottage. I didn't fit in and I knew it. My clothes were wrong; I didn't know what fork to use for what food. I stuck out like a sore thumb."

I flinch as I hear her stark assessment. I'd been oblivious

to most of her discomfort. I'd just been delighted she'd been there at my side.

"Then your dad cornered me. He'd found out my father was getting out of jail. He accused me of not giving a damn about your future. If I cared about you, he said, I'd leave you. He even offered me money to disappear."

She's staring into the distance. "I always knew that my time with you was temporary. I couldn't allow my father to sink his claws in you. So I wrote you a note and left."

"What note?" I ask sharply.

She frowns at me. "The note," she says, as I should know exactly what she's talking about. "You know, where I told you why I was leaving." Her lips twist into a wry smile. "I was young and foolish," she confesses. "I thought you would come after me."

"I never got a note." Waves of pure, cold rage cascade over me. "My father told me he'd offered you fifty thousand dollars to leave me, and you'd accepted."

She stiffens in my embrace. "I didn't take his money."

For nine years, I thought Maddie had picked money over me. My father had played me expertly. Already conditioned to assume that most women were gold-diggers, I'd fallen for his lies and I'd allowed him to ruin the relationship I had with Maddie.

And I might have never known differently. I might have gone to my grave thinking that Maddie had betrayed me.

"I believe you." I swallow. I've been such a fool. I should have known that Maddie would never, ever betray me. "Maddie, I'm so sorry. I listened to my father's lies, and I shouldn't have."

Her eyes sparkle with tears as she squeezes my shoulder. "I'm sorry, too." I start to tell her that this situation isn't her fault, and she holds up her hand. "No, wait, Cam. Let me say this. In the time we dated, you never once made me feel like I didn't belong. You always stood up for me. I should have had more faith in us. I was insecure about being poor, about my dysfunctional family, about my father getting out of jail. I didn't trust what we had between us."

"There's going to be consequences," I vow. "He's never been much of a parent. But," my voice turns to ice, "this time he went too far."

We both fall into silence. I'm simmering in rage. I've tolerated my father's presence in my life, but no longer. If he thinks I'm going to pick my family over Maddie, he's miscalculated. Badly.

It's starting to get dark when we approach the dock. "Not exactly how I'd planned the day," I say wryly to Maddie.

It's the understatement of the year. Today was a fucking disaster. I'd planned on telling her I loved her. I wanted to ask her to stay in Toronto with me.

Instead, I'm left reeling.

She chuckles. "I'd say," she murmurs. She doesn't pull away from my embrace, and I take comfort in that. "Cam," she says, her voice sharper, "is there someone waiting for us at the dock?"

I peer through the gloom. She's right, there's someone pacing up and down. As we near, I make out who it is.

My father.

"Where have you been?" he snaps at me as soon as we're within earshot. "We've been trying to reach you all afternoon."

Tension radiates off Maddie in waves. I fight the urge to punch my father. "What do you want?" I snarl.

His next words cause the bottom to drop out. "Emily had a heart attack," he replies grimly. "She's been airlifted to St. Michael's. The doctors aren't sure if she's going to make it." He gives me a look of sheer contempt. "I hope your *picnic* was worth it."

12

MADDIE

We drive back to Toronto in the dark. Cameron doesn't say a word to me as the miles fly by, and in the quiet, I reflect on the conversation we had today on the boat.

I should be happy. After nine years of wondering why Cameron never reached out to me, I now know the truth. Joseph Drake's lies and manipulation had separated us for almost a decade.

Yet my heart is heavy, and not just because of the horrible news about Emily. On the boat, Cameron and I didn't talk about the future. He didn't ask me to stay in Toronto. When he heard my father was getting out of prison, he didn't respond by reassuring me that we'd solve the problem together.

I've been a fool this week. I've let my hopes cloud my judgment. I knew that letting Cameron back into my life would be dangerous to my heart, and I slept with him anyway.

Worst of all, I fell in love with him once again.

"I didn't see Ryder back at the cottage," I say, breaking the silence that has stretched on for miles. "Did Zoe and he leave for Toronto as well?"

"Does it matter?" His voice is tinged with bitterness. "I hate that cottage. The worst memories of my life are in that place. If it were up to me, I'd raze it to the ground and never look back."

My heart stops. I always knew that my time with Cameron was fleeting. I didn't realize it could end *tonight*. "You don't want to buy the cottage anymore?"

His mouth twists into a grimace. "I never wanted the cottage for myself. Just for Aunt Emily. And now..." His voice trails off. "It might not be an issue anymore."

Despite my best intentions to protect myself, the anguish in his voice almost rips me apart. "She'll make it, Cam." I cover his hand with mine. "She has the best doctors tending to her."

"Anything can happen, Maddie," he replies harshly. His jaw sets in a resolute line. "I have to be prepared for the worst."

My heart breaks for him. "Don't do this to yourself, Cam. Please."

"My mother died of a heart attack," he continues, lost in his musing. "When she was only forty." He lapses back into a brooding silence, and I don't know the right words to help, to pull him out of this dark place that he's fallen into.

"I'll drop you off at the house."

"You don't have to," I reply. "I can take a cab from St. Michael's."

He shakes his head. "Please, Maddie," he says quietly. "I

don't want to worry about you tonight. I just need to know you're safe."

"Okay." Tomorrow, I can begin to pull the pieces of my life back together and figure out how to mend a broken heart. Tonight, Cam's in pain and I'll do anything to make him feel better.

It's too quiet at Cameron's wood and glass home. I swim laps in the swimming pool, under the soft floodlights that illuminate the garden. Even though the exercise leaves me exhausted, it doesn't quell the turmoil in my mind.

Emily might be dying. Cameron and I are ending. It all seems too bleak to contemplate.

Again and again, I drive my drained body until my limbs tremble and my muscles scream with pain. Finally, when it gets to the point when I can't take anymore, I pull myself wearily out of the water, towel off and make my way upstairs.

Cameron's sea-green master bedroom mocks me. The idea of falling asleep on his king-size bed, and waking up to find myself snuggled in his arms... I'm so tempted by the fantasy.

But it's not real.

Don't make things awkward, Maddie. You don't need Cameron to openly reject you to get the message that he's not interested in anything long-term.

I walk past Cameron's bedroom, and make my way to one of his guest bedrooms. I expect to toss and turn, but within an instant of my head hitting the pillow, I'm fast asleep.

WHEN I WAKE UP, Cameron's standing in the doorway. I

blink the sleep out my eyes and turn on the lamp at my side. "What time is it?" I ask, my throat dry and scratchy.

"Four."

He doesn't move. He doesn't say anything else. Dread clutches at my heart. "Emily? Is she okay?"

He nods. "For the moment. The next twenty-four hours are going to be crucial, but the doctors think she's over the worst." He runs his hand through his hair. "You weren't in my bedroom. I thought you'd left."

I don't know how to answer that. I don't know how to respond to the hurt in his voice. I sit up in the bed, forgetting I'd fallen asleep naked. The sheet falls to my waist, exposing my breasts to his gaze.

"Should I leave you alone, Maddie?" he asks me.

Call me foolish, call me selfish, call me stupid. But if things are going to end between us, then I want him one last time. I want to etch the memory of him in my soul.

"No." I lift my eyes to meet his. "Stay with me, Cameron."

He moves to me, intently and forcefully, unzipping his jeans and pulling his t-shirt over his head. I drink in the sight of him, his chiseled body, his dark hair, his blue eyes. "Like what you see, Maddie?"

I kick my blanket off. Holding his gaze, I cup my breasts and run my fingers over my nipples. He inhales sharply. "Like what you see, Cam?"

His lips curl into a grin. "Is that how we're playing?" He fists his length stroking several times, holding my gaze. "Spread your thighs. Touch yourself."

Heat builds in my passage. I part my legs and stroke myself, slowly, softly. My finger traces small circles over my clitoris. I'm picking up speed when I'm startled by his voice. "Stop."

I whimper. He moves closer and places his large hands on my thighs, pushing them wider. "I want you," he says harshly. He places the head of his cock against my pussy. My body aches to deepen the contact, to feel his full, hard length inside me.

His grey-blue eyes hold mine. "What do you need, Maddie?"

"You," I gasp, need stripping all the shyness from me. My eyes are glued to his dick.

"Is that so?" He flexes his hips and slides inside me, another inch. I close my eyes as pleasure spikes through me. Pleasure and frustration, because I want all of him. *Right now.*

He senses the aching void in me. Normally, he'd make me wait, but tonight, he's just as driven as me. "Watch," he says hoarsely, thrusting deep into me.

A cry is torn from me, primal and ragged. "Yes," I hiss out. "Please…"

His mouth descends on my breast, catching a nipple between his teeth. I shiver and moan, writhing beneath his body. "I love the way you look," he murmurs in my ear. "I love the noises you make when I touch you. I love the feel of your skin against mine…"

Another nip of his teeth and I whimper again, my pussy clenching as Cam's thick cock thrusts into me, over and over again. Our lips touch, our tongues dance together. He trails kisses down my jawline, my throat, and my neck. His fingers tweak and pinch my nipples, his hands squeeze my breasts.

His skin slaps against mine, the sound adding to the arousal that hums through my body. At the angle he's thrusting, each stroke hits my g-spot. My insides tighten with the exquisite pressure. "That's it, Maddie," he coaxes. "Let yourself go, love."

The unexpectedness of that endearment pushes me over the edge. I come, shaking and moaning. The muscles in my pussy clench around his cock, and he groans, burying himself deep inside me as he too finds his release.

"What happened with Emily?" I ask him, resting my head on his shoulder. Cam seems more relaxed now, and I take the chance to satisfy my curiosity. "What brought on the heart attack?"

"From the sounds of it, my father was having an argument with my grandfather about money. Emily tried to get in the middle of it, but they yelled at her to stay out of it. That's when she had the attack." He sighs tiredly. "My father's long burned through the trust my grandfather set up for all his children. He's failed at every business he's ever tried to run. He's completely broke. My grandfather didn't tell me exactly what led up to the screaming match, but piecing it together, I'm guessing my father wanted him to invest in his latest cockamamie venture."

"Your father's broke?" I'd have never believed it. Joseph Drake embodies old-money, with his impeccably pressed clothes, his handmade shoes, and his air of barely concealed disdain for most people.

"He's been penniless for years," Cameron confirms. "He lives rent-free in a house I own, and my grandfather gives him a small stipend so he can afford to pay his bills. But the leash is pretty short, and it's about to get shorter." His voice turns grim. "All my life, he's been a terrible role model. He's lied and cheated, he treats people like garbage. With that stunt he pulled with you, he went too far. Once the dust settles, I'm throwing him out."

I want to cheer Cameron's move, but I shiver in fear.

Wounded, cornered animals don't leave the fight; they lash out. Joseph Drake isn't going to back away quietly. I'd wager my last dollar on it.

13

CAMERON

She slept in a guest room.

The last eighteen hours have been filled with turmoil. We haven't had a chance to speak about what really matters. Us. The future. On the boat, I would have sworn that we had one, as soon as I cut my father out of my life. Now, I'm left uncertain once again. Was it just about the money? It can't be.

You have to put your heart on the line, Cameron. You made assumptions once, and it led to nine years of pain. Don't repeat the same mistakes.

"Would you like to come to the hospital?" I ask her as we eat an early morning breakfast. Just cereal and toast, because I'm far too exhausted to cook this morning. I've had less than three hours sleep, and I feel like a zombie. "I called them as soon as I woke up. Aunt Emily woke up briefly last night. They're allowing visitors."

She nods quickly. "That's good news, isn't it?" she asks cautiously. "That they're letting people see her?"

"I think so. Dr. Sharma was optimistic when I spoke to her."

"You spoke to the doctor?" She gulps down the rest of her coffee, and carries the mug to the sink. "Do doctors normally carry on phone conversations with relatives of their patients?"

I shrug. "I donated twenty million dollars to St Michael's last year. I'm sure the money helps."

Her gaze softens. "You did?"

"They had a fundraiser for heart disease."

"And your mother died of a heart attack." She walks up to me. Standing on tiptoe, she kisses me on the cheek. "You're a good person, Cameron Drake."

I wish I was. My father preyed on my fears and separated us. The weight of the guilt I feel my role in the failure of our relationship crushes down on me. *Never again,* I vow silently. Maddie is the most important person in my life. I'm never going to forget it again.

EMILY ISN'T ALONE when we walk in. My grandfather greets Maddie with pleasure, but my father sighs in a long-suffering manner. "The doctors want to limit the visitors to just family," he complains.

"Maddie is family, Joseph," my grandfather snaps with a frown, and my father subsides, quelled for the moment. "Ryder was here earlier," he continues. "You just missed him. He went to the cafeteria to get some coffee."

"I'm sure we'll run into him."

Maddie moves to my aunt's side, inhaling sharply when she takes in Aunt Emily, asleep on the white hospital bed, wires trailing from her arm plugging into softly beeping monitors in the corner of the room. "Her color's better," I reassure her. "You didn't see her yesterday. Trust me, she's definitely showing signs of improvement."

My father nods in agreement. "Dr. Sharma was just in here. She left to do her rounds, but she'll stop by again in a couple hours. Cameron, are you staying?"

I want to have it out with my father, right here, right now, but I hold on to my control. Now is not the time. "We both are." I stifle a yawn. "Is there some place where we can sit?"

"There's a private waiting room next door that they've put at our disposal," my grandfather replies. "If you two are going to be here for a few hours, would you mind if I go home and rest?"

I keep forgetting he's an old man. I watch him walk to the door with unsteady feet, leaning on the walking stick in his hand. "Get some sleep, grandpa," I tell him quietly. "Maddie and I will watch Emily, and we'll call you if something changes."

"I'll come with you, dad," my father says. "I could use some shut-eye myself."

Again, I have to bite back my caustic words with difficulty. My father had only been in the hospital for an hour yesterday, maintaining that it was pointless to sit at Emily's bedside when she was unconscious. He was in bed at eleven. If Joseph Drake is worried for his sister, you wouldn't know it from his behavior.

The two of them leave and Maddie and I settle down in the waiting room. "Cam, I have to ask you something," Maddie blurts out after a few minutes of silence, anxiety writ large on her face. "Do you still want to buy the cottage? Do you still need me to pretend to be your fiancée? Or are we done?"

"I beg your pardon." An outraged voice cuts through the air, and I look up to see my grandfather in the doorway, my father hovering behind him. "You're pretending to be engaged so you can buy the cottage?" My grandfather's face is red with rage. "How dare you, Cameron? How dare you try to swindle me this way? You wanted the cottage so badly that you'd resort to lying to me?"

"Oh my God." Maddie covers her mouth, looking like she's going to be sick. Her face turns white. She rises to her feet, her movement unsteady and jerky. "Cameron," she turns to me with a distraught expression on her face. "I'm so sorry."

It doesn't matter, Maddie. But it's too late. Even as I open my mouth to tell her that I couldn't care less about the cottage, she ducks past my grandfather and my father, and she flees.

"Cameron?" my grandfather repeats, entering the room, his voice icy. "Explain yourself. Did you really hire that woman to impersonate your fiancée?"

"And of all people you could have picked, you chose Maddie Morland?" my father interjects. "What a mistake. That woman is like a leech. Once she gets her claws in you, she'll suck you dry. People like her are only interested in money, Cam. You should know that by now."

My temper, hanging on by a mere thread, snaps. "Shut up," I snarl to my father. "I'll deal with you in a moment." I turn to my grandfather. "Yes, I asked Maddie to pretend to be my fiancée. I had to. You were all set to sell to Ryder, to force your own daughter to move out of her home."

I'm suddenly tired of all the bullshit. "You don't value your own family," I tell him quietly. "Emily sneaked out one night and got in a car accident, and you've punished her all her life because of it. She ceased to matter the instant she defied you."

My grandfather goes white with shock. I'm not done. "And you," I lash out at my father. "God, the fucking apple didn't fall far from the tree, did it? Nine years ago, you drove away the only woman I've ever been in love with. You told me she'd taken your money, and fool that I was, *I believed you*. I fell for every single word."

For too long, I've done the right thing by my family. My grandfather has treated Emily like a second-class citizen her entire life; I've never challenged him. My father's shown me in a thousand ways that he has no moral compass; I've given him a place to live.

I'm through. I care about Aunt Emily, but the rest of my family are on their own. I give my father a withering look. "You had to know there would be consequences if I ever found out the truth. I want you out of my house within the week."

The weight that presses down on me seems to fall away as I cut the cord on my toxic parent. "Sell the cottage to Ryder if you want," I tell my grandfather. "I don't give a damn anymore."

"I don't want it." Ryder's standing in the doorway, an expression of disgust on his face. "I heard the whole sordid thing." He shudders. "My entire life, I had to deal with my father's bullshit. Zoe got pregnant and I thought I could move past it. Children need family, I told myself." He shakes his head vehemently. "No child of mine is going to grow up in such a toxic environment. Cam, I'm sorry. Had I known, I wouldn't have tried to buy the cottage."

"Not your fault." I push the men with only one thought on my mind. I need to find Maddie. She's out there, beating herself up because my grandfather found out about the cottage. I need to tell her I love her. Nothing else matters.

Ryder follows me to the corridor. "I'm really sorry," he repeats. "Find me if you ever need to exchange notes on horrible fathers. Mine cheated on my mother, got another woman pregnant, and never took responsibility for the child, my sister Gigi." There's a pensive look on his face. "Gigi wants nothing to do with the Drakes. I'm beginning to think that she's a lot smarter than I am."

"At this moment, I have to agree with her."

"You love Maddie, don't you?" he asks. "It wasn't just a ruse for the cottage."

"I don't think it was ever a ruse," I confess. "On the surface, I might have convinced myself of that, but deep down..." I swallow the lump in my throat. "Deep down, it was always Maddie. It will always be Maddie."

"Then go after her, man." There's exasperation in his voice. "Why on earth are you here talking to me?"

With heroic effort, I refrain from pointing out to my cousin that he was the one who started the conversation. Giving him a wave, I sprint to the exit.

Glancing into the open door of my aunt's hospital room as I pass it, I notice something that freezes the blood in my veins. My grandfather's slumped in a chair at my aunt's bedside, gazing at his daughter with a troubled expression on his face. *But my father is nowhere to be seen.*

Fuck. Things are bad enough with Maddie. The fate of our relationship rests on a knife's edge. If Joseph Drake managed to sneak out while I was talking to Ryder, there's no telling the damage he might do. And this time around, there won't be any second chances.

14

MADDIE

I've ruined everything.

I run toward the parking lot, my vision blurry from the tears swimming in my eyes. I'm hoping to catch a cab to take me to Cameron's house, then the airport. Unfortunately, there aren't any in sight. Even worse, I have Cam's car keys in my handbag.

I'm not ready to face him. How could I have been that careless? I'd been desperate to know what our future held, but I should have never broached the subject in a public place.

And now I know the answer. We have no future. Not after what just happened.

I open the door of the Porsche and climb in, adding stealing Cameron's car to the list of my sins. I make my plans as I drive to Cameron's Forest Hill house. Most of my belongings are already packed. All I need to do is collect my toiletries and call a cab to take me to the airport. My car is still in Toronto. Cameron arranged for it to be garaged when we were out of town, but I don't know where it is, and I'm too heartsick to figure it out. I just want to leave. With any luck, I can be gone before Cameron notices I'm missing.

Are you really going to run again, Maddie? Haven't you learned anything from last time?

Maybe I have. Maybe what I've learned is that Cameron Drake will break my bruised, aching heart.

I'M WAITING for the cab at the front when a white Audi pulls up and a familiar figure gets out. Joseph Drake.

"What do you want?" It's hard for me to pretend that I don't feel hostility when I look at the man that ruined my relationship with Cameron nearly a decade ago.

"It's not about what I want," he replies. "It's about what you need, Madison. Money."

Oh God. This again.

"Cameron is, as you can probably expect, furious with you," he continues. "Your careless words have ruined his plans to buy the cottage. Whatever deal the two of you had in place, it's over."

"I'll live," I reply tersely. My insides churn as I think of the mounting bills that await me on my return to Calgary. Misti's college tuition, my mother's funeral bills, textbooks, and rent. Even if I work triple shifts at the coffee shop, I'm not going to be able to manage to dig myself out of this hole.

"Will you?" he asks, reading my expression accurately. "Or are you trying to figure out how you'll make ends meet?" He pulls a briefcase from the car and opens it. "Let's lay our cards on the table, Ms. Morland. You have run out of options." He holds out his checkbook. "Except one." His eyes are hard and there's no warmth in his voice. "You aren't the sort of woman I want for my son. Your father is a petty thug with a drug problem and a prison record. Your mother, when she was alive, wasn't any better. Nothing's changed in nine years. Your clothes might be better," his gaze rakes over my outfit dismissively, "but if you put lipstick on a pig, it's still a pig."

He takes a pen from his jacket pocket. "How much will it take?"

Cameron is nowhere to be seen. Joseph Drake is a lying, manipulative man, but in this case, the facts match what he's saying. Cameron didn't talk about the future. He promised me nothing.

I want to believe that what we have is about more than sex, but Cameron never said the words. It's all in my head. My hopes, my dreams, my foolishness. I've wanted Cameron so badly that I've allowed myself to imagine he is in love with me, the way I am with him.

Life rarely offers second chances.

I straighten my spine. "I told you nine years ago, Mr. Drake. My integrity isn't for sale. You tried to pay me off once, and I didn't want your money. Nothing's changed since then. Even if I was drowning in debt, I won't take a dollar from you." My anger bubbles to the surface. "Your lies destroyed our relationship. Cameron might be able to forgive you for it, but I never will."

His gaze falls to the suitcase at my side. "You're leaving," he says. "You think Cameron's going to chase after you? He won't."

I already know that. Cameron might rail against his father, and he might be angry with his grandfather. But he's a Drake. When they're sick, they're assigned private rooms in the hospital with attached waiting areas. They have wings in libraries named after them.

We've always been from different worlds. There has to be an expiry date.

Even as savaged and vulnerable as I feel right now, I'm not going to show this man any sign of weakness. Not after what he's done.

"What I do is none of your business." My voice is tinged with frost. "Why are you here, anyway? Cameron's not happy with you. He wouldn't have sent you."

He draws up, his expression disconcerted.

For the first time, I start using my head instead of reacting with blind instinct. I've struck a nerve with Joseph Drake. *Is it possible that Cameron doesn't know he's here?*

I capitalize on my momentary advantage. "I think you should leave." I pull my phone out of my handbag. "Cam doesn't know where you are, does he? If I had to guess, he'll be extremely angry if he finds out you offered to pay me off. *Again.*" My lips twist into a cold smile. "My relationship with Cameron might not survive today," I tell my nemesis. "Are you certain that yours will?"

He takes another step back. This time, there's definitely fear in his eyes.

"Here's some advice, Mr. Drake. Stay away from me. I'm done being your target. Find someone else to be the pawn in your stupid power games."

His face contorts into a snarl. An hour ago, I'd have been terrified.

Then again, an hour ago, I thought I had something to lose.

Two minutes after Joseph Drake's car pulls away in a cloud of dust, fine gravel and contempt, the taxi arrives. The driver, an older man, gets out and gapes at Cameron's house. "Nice place you have here, miss," he says, looking at the wood and glass structure admiringly. Then he catches sight of Cameron's Porsche and he whistles. "Nice car."

"They aren't mine," I reply flatly. My heart's still pounding in my chest from my confrontation with Cameron's father. I've waited a long time to say those words.

"Is this your luggage?" the man continues genially. "Where are you headed today?"

The words are at the tip of my tongue. *I'm going to the airport. I'm going to catch a flight from Toronto to Calgary, and I'm never coming back.*

But I can't force them past my throat.

Nine years ago, I hadn't trusted Cameron. I hadn't believed in our love and I'd fled in the middle of the night instead of fighting for him.

I'd been wrong. If the events of the last week have proved anything, it's that I never stopped being in love with Cam. I never stopped needing him. That's the reason I didn't date in Calgary, that's the reason I turned down Declan Knight's invitation.

And if I'm being really honest with myself, that's the reason I'm running away now. Putting my heart on the line will *hurt*. Telling Cameron I love him and not hearing it back will destroy me.

But I don't want to spend the next nine years regretting that I didn't have the courage to speak up.

I can't leave without talking to Cameron.

"I'm so sorry." I put my hand on my suitcase to prevent the guy from loading it into the trunk. "I've changed my mind." I dig into my wallet and pull out a twenty-dollar note. *There goes lunch for a week.* "I'm sorry I've wasted your time."

"You don't want to go anywhere?" He mutters something under his breath about inconsiderate rich assholes. Taking the money from me, he stalks back to his cab and drives away.

I watch him leave with vacant eyes, my thoughts far away.

Two years ago, Jenna, Misti, and I had loaded ourselves into a car and had driven three and a half hours to get to Jasper National Park, all because Jenna wanted to walk on the newly opened glass skybridge. The bridge had extended thirty meters from the cliffs, and was three hundred meters above the ground, and I'd been terrified as I inched along it, clinging to the railings for dear life. Every time I caught a glimpse of the ground, far, far below, my insides had lurched with panic. Every time the wind blew, I was convinced I would be hurled off the bridge. When the adventure had ended, I'd sworn I'd never do something that foolhardy again.

Right now, I'd happily walk on that bridge all day if it meant I wouldn't have to face Cameron.

15

CAMERON

It takes me precious minutes to hail a cab. I give the driver my address in Forest Hills, and lean back in the seat. Maddie left twenty minutes ago. She's going to run into the same traffic as us, but because she's driving my car, she'll be less aggressive than the taxi I'm in.

It'll take her a few minutes to pack. With any luck, I'll be able to reach home before she leaves.

Then there's the great X-factor. *My father.* I'm willing to bet the Porsche that he's making trouble. To what end, I have no idea. Does he really think that I'm going to forgive what he did if Maddie leaves?

The car inches forward, making excruciatingly slow progress against Toronto's soul-crushing traffic. Jittery with nerves, I watch the streets, unable to do anything to make the car move faster.

We turn into the side street where I live. I exhale in relief. *Almost there.* Then I see the taxi in the opposing lane, heading away from my house.

It has to be Maddie.

"Follow that cab," I tell my cab driver.

He gives me an *'are you kidding me, buddy'* look in the rear view mirror. I take a hundred dollar bill out of my wallet and hold it up so he can see it. "There's good money in it for you," I tell him. "I need to talk to the passenger in that cab. Can you cut it off?"

The guy's eyes fixate on the bill between my fingertips. "A hundred?" he asks. "Sure, you're the boss." Tires screeching, he takes a highly illegal u-turn, and we're off in pursuit of Maddie.

We're three cars behind as we turn onto Spadina Road. The steady stream of cars coming toward us makes it impossible for us to gain ground. My cab driver shakes his head in frustration. "He'll be harder to catch once we get on Eglinton," he says. "You know where he's going?"

"The airport, probably." Maddie's car is at Drake Media's parking lot. She won't be able to retrieve it without my help.

The man whistles. "If he gets on the highway, we're screwed."

I pull another hundred out of my wallet and hold it up. "It's an emergency."

The second bill doubles my driver's motivation. "Buckle up," he mutters. "I'm going to cut them off at this stop sign."

I wince. I don't want to live without Maddie, but I hadn't planned on dying in a fiery car crash chasing her. Taking heed of the cab driver's suggestion, I fasten my seat belt.

Approaching the four-way stop we speed up and swing into the oncoming lane of traffic. Cars honk and swerve out of the way, and we zoom into the intersection, pulling up in front of the taxi we're chasing.

I'm out of the car in a second, barreling toward the other taxi full tilt, my cab driver on my tail. "Dude, where the fuck's my money?" he yells. I don't respond. I'm staring into the back seat of the car we've just stopped, and it's empty.

"What the fuck is the matter with you?" The driver of the taxi we've cut off gets out and advances in my direction, two hundred and fifty pounds of muscle, irritation radiating from every pore. "Are you fucking stupid? Do you want to get us in an accident?"

An SUV inches past the intersection. The passenger rolls down her window. "I should call 911," she says severely, glaring at both of us. "Toronto traffic is bad enough without idiots like you in it."

I tune it all out. "She's not here," I murmur. "I could have sworn you picked her up."

"What, that chick with the long brown hair?" The driver in front of me rolls his eyes. "That's what this is about? She changed her mind, man. She paid me twenty bucks and sent me away."

My heart hammers in my chest. "She's still there?"

"Unless she called another cab." He peers at me curiously. "Was that your car? Nice wheels, dude."

"Thanks." I apologize to the guy for cutting him off, then turn to my own cab driver. "I seem to have made a mistake," I tell him sheepishly. I pull yet another hundred out of my wallet, because I seem to be passing them around like candy on Halloween.

He takes the notes from me and tucks them into his wallet. "Did anyone tell you you're crazy, dude?" he asks.

"I'm crazy about a girl," I reply. *She's at home. She hasn't left.* "I'm crazy about Maddie."

SHE'S SITTING on one of the deck chairs in the back yard.

She jumps to her feet when she sees me. "I'm so sorry," she starts, then falls silent.

"Hi." My heart hammers in my chest, and I have to force the words out through suddenly nerveless lips. I'm so desperately in love with Maddie. "I'm Cameron." I swallow. God, this seemed like a much better idea in the cab. "I swim too."

Her brow furrows. "What are you talking about?"

"Catch on, Mads." Exasperation tinges my voice. "Big romantic moment here. Let's try this again." I stick my hand out in greeting and repeat the words I'd used when I met her for the first time. "Hi, I'm Cameron. I swim too."

Her lush lips curve into a grin as she figures out what I'm doing. She takes my hand. "I'm Maddie," she replies, her eyes twinkling the way they had ten years ago. "We're in a swim meet. I assumed you swim. Tell me something I don't know."

Ten years back, I'd told her I thought she had the prettiest eyes. It's still true, but this time around, I have something better to say. "I can predict the future."

"You can?"

I nod. "We're going to fall in love, and we're going to date for a year, but we're going to break up because of a stupid misunderstanding." I look into her eyes. "That's not the end of the story though."

"It isn't?" Her voice is very soft.

"No." I shake my head and take her hands in mine. "We find each other again. We pretend to be engaged. And," I look into those beautiful hazel eyes, "I fall in love with you. All over again."

She makes a noise that's half-squeak, half-whimper. I take that as a good sign. "I'm absolutely, crazily, madly in love with you, Madison Morland. If you need me to move to Calgary, I will. I'll do anything. I love you and I don't want to lose you ever again."

She steps toward me, her eyes shining. "I love you too, Cam. So much so that I don't have the words for it."

I close my eyes and hold her, feel the warmth of her, breathe in her softness. "What happened to the cottage?" she asks. "Is your grandfather angry?"

"Ryder doesn't want it anymore. I have a feeling things will work out just fine."

"Good." She's silent for a few minutes. "I thought you didn't want me," she confesses, her voice soft.

"What on earth?"

"You didn't say anything."

She's right. I mean, I'd argue until I'm blue in the face that actions speak louder than words, and she should have known that I was crazy about her, but now is really not the time. "I love you," I repeat. "I want to spend the rest of my life with you."

"My father is going to ask you for money," she warns me. "Your father hates me. This isn't going to be easy."

"I don't care. We'll handle it. We can handle anything together."

A yawn overtakes me, and she immediately pulls away, her expression concerned. "You haven't slept at all. Is someone keeping a watch on Emily?"

"Ryder and Noah."

"Good. Go straight to bed."

"Bossy, aren't we?" I raise an eyebrow. "I'll go to bed if you'll join me."

She mock-frowns as she links her arm in mine. "I know that look," she scolds. "You need sleep, not sex."

My hand trails suggestively down her backside. "Are you sure, baby? I've got moves, you know."

Her breath catches when she sees the heat in my eyes. We head upstairs, hand in hand.

Sleep? Sleep can wait. Today is the first day of the rest of our lives and I'll be damned if I'm going to waste it.

16

MADDIE

One year later...

It's a beautiful Friday afternoon. After a week of non-stop rain, the weather's finally cleared up. The sky is periwinkle blue and there's not a cloud in sight. Of course, the traffic on the 400 is stop-and-go, but like they say, you win some, you lose some.

Cam hates being stuck in traffic, so I'm behind the wheel of the Porsche. If I drive, I thought, at least I won't have to hear him bitch about idiot drivers who don't tie down their canoes properly.

I didn't realize that there would be another benefit.

Cam's fingers trail down my arm. "I like this dress," he says, his eyes lingering appreciatively on my cleavage. My insides clench at his fiery gaze. "Blue's a good color on you."

His fingers move from my arms to my thighs. The sundress has ridden up almost to mid-thigh, leaving my legs bare and exposed. His voice deepens as he caresses my skin. "Did you do as I asked?"

No panties, he'd ordered with a wicked gleam in his eye.

If I have to be stuck in traffic, you're going to make it worth my while.

"Maybe," I reply, keeping my tone nonchalant. "Maybe not."

His lips turn up in a grin. "There's only one way to find out for sure…" he says, his tone teasing. He slides his hand between my inner thighs, and I inhale sharply as he touches me with whisper-soft strokes.

"Cam," I warn him, as a familiar need fills my body, "I'm driving your car. You don't want me to crash it."

"It's just a car," he says with a smile. "Surely you know that by now, Mads."

I look at the man at my side, love overflowing in my heart. I'd given up on dating, given up on finding someone that ever made me feel. Then I found Cam again, and I discovered what happily-ever-after feels like.

And it feels amazing.

Misti is in her junior year in college. Cameron offered to pay for her to go to school in Toronto, but she declined. I think she's seeing someone in Calgary, but she won't tell me what's going on. I'm not too worried; she's roommates with Jenna, who'll keep her out of trouble. The two of them are flying in tomorrow to spend a week with us at the cottage. I see the two of them fairly often--Cam makes sure of it--but I still miss my baby sister.

As I'd foreseen, my father tried to wheedle money out of Cam. We refused. "We'll pay for rehab, if you'll go," I told him. He called me an ungrateful brat who thought she was too good for her family. We haven't been in touch since. Somewhat predictably, he is back in jail, this time for a parole violation.

Things are more complicated with Cam's family.

When Cam found out about his father's latest attempt to

pay me off, he evicted him from the house and cut him out of his life. Cameron's grandfather is still in contact with Joseph Drake, as is Emily, but I haven't seen Cameron's father for a year now.

I would like to pretend that I want Cam to be reunited with his father, but I can't lie. Joseph Drake has never apologized for what he did, and until he does, Cameron won't entertain any suggestion of a reconciliation.

While Cameron's relationship with his father has eroded, his relationship with his grandfather has strengthened. Edward Drake had been horrified when Cameron pointed out how he'd treated his paralyzed daughter. Once Emily had regained consciousness, the two of them had a long heart to heart. None of us know the particulars of that conversation, but the cottage isn't for sale anymore, not to Ryder, Cameron or anyone else. Edward Drake rewrote his will to ensure that on his death, Emily will inherit the cottage that is so dear to her heart.

Once that decision was made, tensions decreased dramatically and the family started to heal. The cottage has become a place of warmth, fun and laughter. We spent Thanksgiving there last year, and had a surprisingly wonderful time.

"Penny for your thoughts, Maddie."

Cameron's fingers are just inches away from my clitoris. My nipples harden and my muscles tense in anticipation of his touch.

God, I'm lucky.

BY THE TIME we get to the cottage, stars are shining in the night sky. Ryder, Zoe, and baby Charlotte are there already, as is Emily and her caregiver Jenny.

Ryder and Cameron greet each other cordially. I hug Emily and Zoe and coo over Charlotte. "She's become so big," I marvel, picking up the nine-month old. "Look at her."

"She's crawling now," Zoe says. "She's a little menace."

I cuddle the baby. "When's Edward getting in?"

"In the morning," she replies. "Noah's bringing him up. Your sister is on her way too, isn't she?"

I nod, only half-listening to Zoe. Cameron stretches languidly, his t-shirt riding up, exposing his hard abs, and I ogle shamelessly. *Mmm.*

Zoe says something to me, and I don't catch a single word. "Sure," I reply vaguely, and she bursts into a peal of laughter.

"Maddie," she teases me. "Do you know what you just agreed to do?"

Oh dear. I move Charlotte's little fist away from my earrings and give Zoe a rueful look. "I wasn't listening," I confess, stating the obvious.

Her lips twitch. "Because you were too busy checking out Cameron."

Cameron hears us. "You ladies talking about me?" His eyebrow lifts. "Should I be flattered or afraid?"

"Flattered," Zoe giggles. "So, you guys, have you eaten dinner? There are leftovers in the fridge."

I'm about to reply that I'm starving, but Cameron shakes his head. "Maddie and I were going to take a walk," he says.

We are? I give Cam a puzzled stare, but he avoids my gaze. "Right," I murmur, my heart lurching.

We head outside. A full moon shines down on us, and the water laps at the shore in silvery waves. The night air is warm and balmy. Holding hands, we walk along the tree-lined pathway to the dock. Cameron is quiet. "Is everything alright?" I ask him, a little nervous at the way he's acting.

"Between us?" He bumps my shoulder companionably. "Of course, Maddie. Why wouldn't it be?"

"Because you're being a little weird?"

His teeth flash in the dark. "Nice night, don't you think?"

We reach the shimmering lake. Normally, I'd kick off my flip-flops and wade into the water, but right now, I'm too exasperated with Cam. "Cut it out," I tell him, turning toward him, but freeze when I notice he's down on one knee and he's holding a ring in his hand. The same ring he gave me before.

Oh. My. God.

"Maddie," Cameron says, "Ten years ago, I saw this ring in an antique store, and I knew it was perfect for you." He swallows. "When we broke up, I couldn't bear to get rid of it. I put it in a box, and I thought I could forget. And then you came back into my life."

My eyes fill with tears. There's some sadness for the years we spent apart, but mostly, they're happy tears. Against all odds, we found each other again.

"I love you, Maddie. I want to spend the rest of my life with you. Laughing with you, loving you. Will you marry me?"

"Yes," I squeak out, giddy with joy. I sink down on my knees and throw my arms around him, almost knocking him off balance. The two of us collapse in a laughing heap on the deck, my body on top of his. "I love you, Cam."

Cam puts his arm around my waist, and tightens his grip. His voice dances with amusement. "I'm going to take that as a yes on the proposal."

I kiss him, molding my body against his, feeling his erection against my thigh. He slides the ring on my finger. Closing my eyes, I take a deep breath. This feels so right. Like coming home.

"Yes," I whisper. "That's definitely a yes on the proposal."

Last year, when Cameron gave me this ring, I was terrified about the future. Not anymore. Now, all I can feel is joy that I get to spend the rest of my life with this man. We waited nine years for our happily-ever-after. I snuggle into the arms of the man I love. "I think we should celebrate," I mutter, moving my body closer to his.

He chuckles, reading my mind perfectly. "Here on the dock? Anyone could walk by at any moment."

"True." Reluctantly, I abandon my thoughts of jumping him, disentangle myself from his grip and clamber to my feet.

"Shall we head to the bedroom?" he continues with a wicked gleam in his eyes. "Like you said, we do need to celebrate."

I grin at him, wide and happy, and look at the ring he slipped on my finger.

Against all odds, we got a second chance. This time, I'm not letting Cameron go. This time, it's real and it's forever.

Thank you for reading Cameron and Maddie's story! I hope you love them as much as I do.

WANT MORE ROM-COM? If you enjoyed Fake Fiance, may I recommend checking out my contemporary romance story MAX? It's a friends-to-lovers romance that's lighthearted and funny. Flip the page for an extended preview of MAX.

Do you enjoy fun, light, contemporary romances with lots of heat and humor? Want to read *Boyfriend by the Hour (A Romantic Comedy)* for free? Want to stay up-to-date on new releases, freebies, sales, and more? (There will be an occasional cat picture.) **Sign up to my newsletter!** You'll get the book right away, and unless I have a very important announcement—like a new release—I only email once a week.

A PREVIEW OF MAX BY TARA CRESCENT

She put me in the friend-zone. I want out.

Rule #1: *Never hook up with a woman who is looking for a relationship.*
Rule #2: *Always do breakups in a public space.*

I have a reputation.

I'm a player. Three dates and I'm out.

I don't do commitment. My idea of a romantic evening involves making a woman cry out in toe-curling, window-shattering pleasure.

Until I meet Charlie.

She's beautiful. She's funny and she's feisty.

And she's put me straight in the friend-zone.

I shouldn't care, but with Charlie? I'm playing for keeps.

∽

CHAPTER 1

Max:

I should never have broken Rule Number One. *Don't hook up with a woman who is looking for a relationship.*

In my defense, I didn't know Abby was looking for a boyfriend. We met in a bar. I'd just finished a set. She bought me a drink and asked if I was doing something later that night. "Hopefully, you," I said, and despite the horrible pickup line, we ended the evening at her place.

So far, so good, right? *Wrong.*

Three dates later, Abby wants to be in a relationship. She's asked me if I have plans for the Labor Day weekend. She's hinted that she'd like to meet my parents. The other night, she came over and watched a romantic comedy on my couch.

It's time for Abby to go. Call me an asshole if you must, but I don't make romantic weekend plans. I don't take women home to meet the family, and my apartment will forever remain a Jennifer Aniston-free zone.

Which brings me to Rule Number Two. *Always do breakups in a public space.* It's much easier and cleaner that way.

Opposite me, Abby's eyes brim with tears. "But we had a connection, Max," she wails. "My psychic even said you were the one."

Oh for fuck's sake. Insert eye-roll. "You have a psychic that you take relationship advice from?"

Heads swivel to look at me. *Shit. That came out louder than I intended.* The blonde sitting at the table next to me looks up, and at the bar, Joe frowns in my direction and gives me his patented *'don't cause a scene, asshole'* glare.

Causing a scene is the last thing I want to do. I'm a big fan of *uncomplicated*. "Abby," I say, holding up my hands in a placating gesture. "Come on, I've been honest with you from the start. I'm not looking for anything serious. You want casual sex? I'm your guy. But that's all I'm interested in."

"Why?" she sniffs. "Don't you want a family, kids?"

"No." My reply is instantaneous. My primary focus right now is getting my small baking business off the ground. Even if I wanted one, I don't have time for a relationship.

Abby glares at me and her voice rises to a pitch. "You're just not giving me a chance."

Clingy women make me want to run. The blonde looks amused, but Joe's still scowling. "Abby," I repeat gently, resisting my urge to flee, and wishing that Joe would swing by with another beer, "I'm really sorry."

"Fine," she snarls, pushing her chair back with a loud scrape, and rising to her feet. "I'm out of here." She pivots on her heels and starts to flounce out, then she swings back and fixes me with an accusing look. "It's all fun and games for you, isn't it? One day, things are going to be different. You're going to fall in love, Max, and I only wish I could be there to see the train wreck."

She exits in a snit, and I lean back in my seat and drain the pint in front of me. The blonde's still looking at me. "What are you looking at?" I snap. "You want to tell me what a horrible person I am too? Fine. Knock yourself out."

She chuckles. "Max, right?" she asks. "I don't think you're a horrible person." She gets to her feet, her brown eyes twinkling with amusement. "But your breaking-up skills could use a lot of work." Her lips quirk up. "Hopefully, you have other talents."

Wait a second - who is this woman?

She walks over to the bar, and tosses a twenty on the counter. "See you next week, Joe?" she says. "Oh, and hey, buy Max a beer for me, will you? He's having a rough night."

Joe takes a look at my face and laughs out aloud. "Sure thing, Charlie."

She turns to leave and I finally react, scrambling to my feet and joining her at the bar. "You're not going to stay?"

"Oh no, Max. You're not my type."

Once she's gone, I turn to Joe. "Who was that?" I ask him, a bit dazed from the encounter.

Joe pushes a beer in front of me. "That's Charlie Campbell. She's a regular as well. Uses the bar for the same reason as you do."

"As a public venue to break up with someone?"

"Exactly." Joe smirks at me. "Charlie and you, you guys are like two peas in a pod. I should have introduced you to each other much earlier."

"Dude," I protest, settling myself on the barstool and taking a deep swig of my drink. "I'm nothing like that woman. I'm not cocky and arrogant."

"What the fuck are you talking about, Max? Of course you are." He grins. "This is going to be so much fun."

CHAPTER 2

Charlie:

In general, I've good taste in guys.

Not so Richard. So far, I've gone out with him three times. In that brief period, he's insulted me, every waiter who's served us, all the wineries in Argentina and right now, he's on a rant about Joe's bar. Insult me all you want, but when you start on Joe? *Crossing a line.*

All I want is a restful evening. One of my current cases is a nightmare. Single mom breaks up a fight between her kid and some rich teenager, and the teenager's parents have her arrested for assault. It should have been an easy dismissal, but the kid's parents are determined to drag Renee through the mud. And if I can't win this case, Renee faces six years in jail, and her kid gets shunted into the foster care system. The whole thing is awful.

"Richard," I lean forward, interrupting a monologue about Malbec. I've made up my mind - I don't have time for this bullshit. Life is too short to spend with boorish men. "Listen, I don't think we should see each other anymore."

His face turns red. "What?"

"I said, I don't think we should see each other anymore."

Right then, Max walks into the bar, and I feel my face break out into a smile. Every time I've thought about our encounter three weeks ago, I've had to grin. Yeah, I was a little ballsy with him, but I couldn't resist. Max is tattooed, bearded and ripped, and he just oozes charm and self-assurance. He was practically begging me to mess with him.

"You're breaking up with me?" Richard's voice rises, and his face takes on an unpleasant scowl. "Are you fucking kidding me? Runaway Charlie Campbell. They warned me about you, and rather than listen, I gave you a chance."

Gee thanks, asshole. Max's chatting with Joe, the two of

them laughing about something. Two dimples flash on his cheeks when he smiles. *Seriously adorable.* It takes effort to tear my gaze away from him and back to Richard.

"Let's not make a scene, okay?"

"Fuck you, bitch," he snaps. "Don't tell me what to do." His fingers dig into my upper arm. "You think you can just waltz in and out of people's lives without consequences?"

"Umm, yes, I do?" I try to shake free of his grip, but he's stronger than me. "I don't know if you've noticed, Richard, but we live in a free country, which means that after three dates, if I decide I don't want a fourth, I've the right to say no."

"You fucking cunt." His voice is a low snarl, and there's hatred in his eyes. He pulls me toward him. "You are going to regret this."

Oh my god, this guy is unravelling at the idea that I'm breaking up with him. He's some kind of investment banker - I guess women usually don't say *no* to him? Yikes. Right now, he's projecting sexual predator, and I'm really, *really* glad that I've always ended relationships in the relative safety of Joe's bar.

"Let me go, Richard." I'm proud at how calm I sound.

"Or what?"

"Or you'll be sorry, asshole," a cool voice cuts in. Max is at my side, looming threateningly over Richard. "I believe the lady told you to let her go." His hands are clenched into fists at his side. "If I were you, I'd listen."

Richard takes one look at Max and reconsiders his stand, releasing my arm without further comment. Max's eyes fall to my reddened skin. "Are you okay, Charlie?" he asks, his voice gentle.

I nod silently. Now that the moment has passed, I can feel my heart pounding in my chest. "I'm fine."

"I'm escorting you out of here." Max turns to face Richard, his expression hard and his voice layered with rage. "And I'm warning you. You ever come within three feet of this woman again, and you'll regret it."

My hands are still shaking as I settle at the bar. Joe's over in an instant. "That didn't look pleasant," he says, his casual words not quite hiding the real concern in his tone. "Who's the jerk?"

"He works in the building next to mine," I say tonelessly, gulping down the scotch Joe's placed in front of me. "We kept running into each other at the Korean noodle place in the lobby. Damn it, I'll have to find a new bibimbap place." I frown into my drink. "Asshole."

"Indeed." Max comes back in and takes a seat next to me. His gaze runs over me, and he notices the tremble in my fingers that I can't quite conceal. "Your date's a prick, Charlie."

I laugh shakily. "You won't hear any argument from me there," I agree. "I guess he thought that if he bought me three dinners, I was obligated to put out."

Max frowns. "Does the guy know where you live? Does he have a key to your place?"

"No." My mood improves as I see another opportunity to tease Max. "Do you give women keys to your place after three dates?" I can't help grinning at him. "I didn't think of you as the commitment-seeking type."

Joe, who's listening to our conversation, snorts at that. "Max give a girl a key to his place?" He rolls his eyes. "This guy? Three dates is Max's limit."

"Seriously?"

"Let me guess, Charlie," Max challenges lightly, those dimples flashing into view. "You're searching for your soulmate, right?"

Not even a little. I ignore the question directed at me. "So what happens after the third date? You can't get it up?"

Joe bursts out laughing. Max tries to look wounded, but he can't maintain a straight face for very long. "I thought you were on my side," he grumbles to Joe, before turning to me with a wry grin. "I assure you, Charlie, I've never had any complaints."

He's so cute. Okay, cute's not a great way to describe a grown man, but he's got a Chris Pratt vibe going on. Add in those dimples, and he's irresistible.

And as tempting as it is to snack on this piece of man-candy, I resist. I love this bar and I love Joe. I've been coming here at least once a week for the better part of a year and a half. This has become a place of sanctuary to me. Max is clearly friends with Joe, and is probably a regular here as well. You know what they say - *you don't shit where you eat.*

I change the topic. "Thank you for coming to my rescue. How did you know I was in trouble?"

His eyes twinkle. "The last time you were here, Charlie," he drawls, "you told me that my break-up skills needed work." His lips compress with mirth. "I was watching you, hoping to pick up a tip or two."

I flip him off, but the gesture has no heat. "Let me buy you a drink," he continues. "And Charlie," he looks at me with a wicked glint in his eyes, "you are most definitely my type."

He's rescued me from Richard and now he's flirting with me. My insides liquefy as I contemplate the idea of his big hands running all over my body, squeezing my breasts, snaking lower to find my heat...

Stop that, Charlie.

"Max," I shake my head sternly, "I'm not going to start something with you. Neither of us do relationships, so when we implode, we'd have to determine who gets custody of Joe's bar."

"Me." He doesn't try to deny that we'll implode. "I went to high school with Joe."

"And I've been coming here for the last eighteen months."

"Stop fighting, you two," Joe instructs, moving back to us after serving a couple of customers. "If you want to avoid a clusterfuck, don't sleep together. Surely, even for the two of you, that's possible."

"Of course it is," we both say at the same time, then we grin at each other. Max cocks his head to one side and sticks his hand out. "Friends?"

My libido mutters a protest, and I ignore it ruthlessly. Sex isn't necessary, and having a bar to call home is a lot more important. I put my hand in his, ignoring how good his touch feels, ignoring the shock of desire that travels up from the point of contact through my entire body. "Friends."

Click to keep reading MAX: A Friends to Lovers Romance. It's a standalone romance with a guaranteed HEA and absolutely no cheating!

A NOTE FROM TARA

Dear readers,

I hope you enjoyed reading *Fake Fiance*.

Would you help me out by leaving a review? Reviews are hugely important in helping readers decide on their next book. Please take a moment to tell me what you thought — I'd really, really appreciate it.

If you'd like to be stay informed about what I'm working on, and get notified when my books go on sale or when I publish a new book, please do sign up to my mailing list. As a special bonus, you also get a free story for subscribing.

You can also follow me on Amazon. Click here to get to my author page, and on the left hand side, there's a yellow Follow button (right below the author picture).

You won't receive sale notifications that way (I think), but you will find out about new releases.

Cheers and happy reading!

Tara

ABOUT TARA CRESCENT

Get a free story from Tara when you sign up to Tara's mailing list.

Tara Crescent writes steamy contemporary romances for readers who like hot, dominant heroes and strong, sassy heroines.

When she's not writing, she can be found curled up on a couch with a good book, often with a cat on her lap.

She lives in Toronto.

Tara also writes sci-fi romance as Lili Zander. Check her books out at http://www.lilizander.com

Find Tara on:
www.taracrescent.com
taracrescent@gmail.com

ALSO BY TARA CRESCENT

CONTEMPORARY ROMANCE

The Drake Family Series

Temporary Wife (A Billionaire Fake Marriage Romance)

Fake Fiance (A Billionaire Second Chance Romance)

Standalone Books

Hard Wood

MAX: A Friends to Lovers Romance

A Touch of Blackmail

A Very Paisley Christmas

Boyfriend by the Hour

MÉNAGE ROMANCE

Club Ménage

Menage in Manhattan

The Dirty series

The Cocky series

Dirty X6

BDSM ROMANCE

Assassin's Revenge

Nights in Venice

Mr. Banks (A British Billionaire Romance)

Teaching Maya

The House of Pain

The Professor's Pet

The Audition

The Watcher

Doctor Dom

Dominant - *A Boxed Set containing The House of Pain, The Professor's Pet, The Audition and The Watcher*

You can also keep track of my new releases by signing up for my mailing list!

Printed in Dunstable, United Kingdom